# WOLF
## in
# SHEEP'S
# CLOTHING

# WOLF

## in

# SHEEP'S
# CLOTHING

*A Garth Ryland Mystery*
## JOHN R. RIGGS

DEMBNER BOOKS New York

Dembner Books
Published by Red Dembner Enterprises Corp.,
80 Eighth Avenue, New York, N.Y. 10011
Distributed by W. W. Norton & Company, Inc.,
500 Fifth Avenue, New York, N. Y. 10110

**Library of Congress Cataloging-in-Publication Data**
Riggs, John R., 1945–
Wolf in sheep's clothing / John R. Riggs.
    p.   cm. — (A Garth Ryland mystery)
    ISBN 0-942637-16-X : $16.95
    I. Title.   II. Series: Riggs, John R., 1945–  Garth Ryland
mystery.
PS3568.I372W64   1989
    813'.54--dc19
                                            89-30968
                                            CIP

*Design by Antler & Baldwin, Inc.*

To Carole, For every reason.

 *1*

Sometimes a feeling just won't let you go. I awakened at first light, looked at my watch and groaned, rolled over and lay perfectly still, pretended to sleep. I didn't fool anyone. Not the birds who began to chirp right outside my bedroom window. Not the neighbor's dog who had a squirrel treed on my porch roof. Not the sun which went right on rising without me. Not myself. I went downstairs to put on a pot of coffee.

While waiting for the coffee to perk, I used some cold hard logic to try to put the feeling to rest. Diana was fine. She'd gone weeks without writing before, and nothing had been wrong. Why, then, did it matter that I hadn't heard from her within the past three weeks, or that she was over a week late in getting home from her trip up north with Devin LeMay? That in itself wasn't anything to worry about. Still, I worried every time I

1

thought about the phone conversation we'd had a few days before she left.

"Are you alone?" I'd called her at her apartment in Madison and waited through several rings before she answered. Usually that meant she wasn't alone.

"Who is this?" she'd asked sharply.

"It's Garth. Ruth said you'd called earlier and for me to call back."

"Garth! You don't know how good it is to hear from you," she said.

"Likewise, I'm sure." That said, I sat down on the threshold between the kitchen and the dining room, and in the silence that followed, listened to the refrigerator hum.

"I don't quite know how to begin," she finally said.

"I have all night," I answered.

"It might take that long."

I had known Diana for seven years, ever since I'd bought the *Oakalla Reporter* and come back to Oakalla to live. From the beginning we were friends. I eventually came to spend my Saturday mornings at her house, drinking coffee and eating doughnuts, while she painted. It didn't matter whether we talked or not. I just liked being in the same room with her, watching her work, and giving her my opinion whenever she asked for it. And I'd better give her my honest opinion. She could smell a lie a mile off.

Then two years and four months ago her husband (and my friend) Fran committed suicide. Soon after that Diana and I became lovers. In August of that year she enrolled in the University of Wisconsin at Madison and had recently completed an M.A. in Art there. While there, she met an English professor named Devin LeMay, and they, too, became, and remained, lovers.

2

Then a few months ago she'd put her house up for sale, and it had just sold to a retired schoolteacher. Looking back at Diana and me, I wished we had done some things differently, even though I once vowed I would never look back on any part of my life and say, I wish. I wished we had gone on being friends, instead of becoming lovers so soon after Fran died, because from then on the fun and playfulness seemed to go out of our friendship. We spent most of our time together talking about us, analyzing our feelings and trying to make them fit our lives, instead of just being, doing, laughing, and playing as we had before. We lost something else at that time as well—our naturalness, or whatever it is that enables two people completely to relax in each other's company and be themselves without pretext or regret. We became too close guardians of each other's feelings, and tried too hard to please.

I also wished that Devin LeMay had never come into Diana's life, and that I could make it through a single day without thinking about Diana and him. I wished that I could hold her in my arms the way I used to and that I'd never again wake up in pain, then roll over in bed and hug my pillow.

"You know I've sold my house," she said.

"I've heard rumors."

"Well, they're true." Another pause.

"Did you get what you were asking?" I asked.

"Close enough so that I couldn't turn it down."

"I would have turned it down."

"I know," she answered. "Sometimes I think you love that house more than I do."

"At least as much," I agreed.

"Then why didn't you make an offer on it?"

"Because I couldn't afford it."

"I see."

3

The refrigerator shut down as the crickets began to chirp outside. You can supposedly tell the temperature by counting how many times a cricket chirps a minute, adding his body weight, minus his left-handed first cousins, then multiplying by the number of black sheep in Farmer Brown's pasture. But I never had the patience to count cricket chirps.

"So what are you going to do now?" I asked.

"As soon as I can get packed, I'm moving to New Mexico."

"To do what?"

"Draw, paint, whatever I feel like doing. Devin says the earth vibrations are really good there."

"Is that supposed to convince me that you belong there?"

She laughed. "No. I just thought I'd throw that in. I know how you are about the psychic feelings some people get."

"I don't deny they happen," I said. "They've just never happened to me."

"I know that, too."

"Is Devin going along?" I asked.

"No." She was certain. "Devin and I have reached that point . . . Well, you know what I mean."

"Have you told him that?"

"No. I've been waiting for the right time."

"Which is when?"

"I don't know for sure. I'm thinking I'll have my chance next week," she said. "We're taking a short vacation together."

That hurt. I'd been hoping for some time that Diana and I could take a vacation of our own. "Where are you and Devin going?" I asked.

"Up north somewhere. One of Devin's former students has invited us up to his cabin in Minnesota."

"Where in Minnesota?"

"I don't remember for sure. To be honest, I really don't care. If it weren't for Devin, I wouldn't even go."

"Then why are you?"

"I hate to disappoint him," she said. "He's so like a little boy when he gets his heart set on something. It's hard to say no to him."

I let that ride. Discussions of Devin LeMay usually didn't bring out the best in me. "No other reason for going up there with him?" I asked.

She hesitated before she answered. "No. No other reason." But she didn't quite convince either one of us.

"When do you think you'll be back from there?"

"In no more than a week. We leave Friday, and Devin starts orientation a week from next Monday, so we'll have to be back by then. Besides that, I've got to start packing sometime soon."

"Fair enough," I said.

"Why did you want to know?"

"I hoped we'd have time to take a trip somewhere before you left. But that seems out of the question now."

"Garth! Why didn't you say something?" she replied. "You don't know how I'm dreading this trip with Devin."

"Then don't go."

"It's not that simple," she said.

"Why isn't it?"

Again I waited for her answer. "It's just not, that's all. And I really don't want to discuss it."

"Diana?" I said before she could hang up. "When you answered the phone, you sounded unsure of yourself, maybe a little frightened. Does it have anything to do with the trip you're about to take with Devin?"

5

"No," she answered. "Just somebody's idea of a joke."

"What is?"

"The obscene phone calls. They come at all hours, though usually late at night. My guess is it's junior high kids, calling when their parents are gone."

"Why junior high kids?" The crickets had quit chirping. I wondered if it had reached zero outside.

"Their voices. They sound boyish to me."

"*Their* voices." I was relieved. With obscene phone calls, there was usually safety in numbers.

"*His* voice," she admitted. "But there could be more than one."

"What does his voice sound like?" I asked.

"Boyish, like I said before. And . . ." She didn't finish.

"And what?"

"Cold," she replied. "Very cold and calculating."

"But not a man's voice?"

"No. I'm sure of that."

"What in particular does he say to you?" I asked.

"You don't want to know. Let's just say he starts with whore and goes from there."

"What do you say in return?"

"Nothing. I hang up as soon as I'm sure it's he."

"Any ideas who he is?"

"No. That's why I think it's kids calling at random." She paused. "At least in the beginning I did."

My ears pricked up. "Why not now?"

"Things he says. Personal things. It's almost like he knows me."

"But you don't know him?" I wanted to make sure.

"No. I'm absolutely certain of that."

"Have you told the police?"

"No. I figure I'll be out of my apartment in a couple weeks. Then it'll be somebody else's problem."

"In that case I hope a ten-foot gorilla moves in."

"That or a black belt."

"Poetic justice either way." I searched for just the right thing to say, but it never came to me. "Take care of yourself." I said with more finality than I intended.

"Always," she answered with the same finality. "And drop me a postcard when you get wherever you're going."

"I'll be sure to."

"Diana . . ."

"Yes?"

"Nothing. I love you."

"I love you too."

"Good-bye, then."

"Good-bye."

The receiver slid from my hand and landed in its cradle. I tried to call her back, but already her line was busy. I tried again an hour later, got the same results, and went to bed thinking I should warn her about something, though I didn't know what. Three weeks later her postcard had yet to arrive. Neither had she called to tell me she was home. Every day I knocked on her door in the hope that she would answer. Every day I felt a rock within me harden.

"Don't you ever sleep?" Ruth came into the kitchen wearing her flowered pink robe and Band-Aids on both big toes to cover the blisters from her new bowling shoes. A widow who had buried her only two children along with her beloved husband, Karl, Ruth had seen it all in her sixty-some years, so nothing really surprised her. Though, as she'd been quick to point out on more than one occasion, somehow I always found new ways of testing that theory. We'd been together for seven years, ever since she'd answered my ad in the *Oakalla Reporter* for a live-in housekeeper. With luck, patience, and humor we'd managed to survive those seven years. And somewhere along the line, though neither of us knew when, we'd become friends.

Ruth turned down the fire under the coffee, which had started to boil over onto the stove. "You look a wreck," she said.

"Thanks. I feel like one."

"Do you want to eat breakfast before you tell me about it?"

"What are you planning on fixing?"

"Ham and scrambled eggs." Having spent nearly all of her life on a farm, Ruth couldn't fix a cold breakfast no matter how hot it was outside.

"I can live with that."

She put a black iron skillet on the stove. "It wasn't multiple choice to begin with." After pouring us each a cup of coffee, she cut a slice of ham and laid it in the skillet. Meanwhile I added sugar and half-and-half to my coffee, then tasted it to see how well I'd done. Grandmother Ryland once told me there was no such thing as too strong coffee, only too weak men. Watching my spoon dissolve into my cup, I had the feeling Grandmother Ryland would have approved.

"This is the fourth morning in a row you've been up with the chickens," Ruth observed. "So whatever it is, it must not be getting any better."

"It's Diana," I said. "I'm worried about her."

"It's not the first time." Not tolerant to begin with, Ruth was least patient where Diana was concerned.

"This is different," I said.

"How different?"

"I can't explain it. Just a feeling I have that she

8

might be in danger. There's probably nothing to worry about, but still I'm worried."

Ruth sliced another piece of ham, but left it on the cutting board. Judging by the look on her face, something was worrying her, too. "Maybe you have reason," she said.

"What do you mean?"

"Nothing," she said, laying the ham in the skillet.

Later, as we sat across the table from each other, our plates empty and a second cup of coffee in our hands, Ruth was still preoccupied. I'd described Diana's obscene phones calls and mentioned that she was a week overdue on her return from up north, but neither item seemed to make much of an impression on Ruth. Like a bulldog with a bone, she had fastened on something and wouldn't let go.

"A penny for your thoughts," I said.

"No comment," she said.

"Is it about Diana?"

She rose and began to clear the table. "I said no comment."

"That's your final answer?"

To make her point, she went into the bathroom, and closed then locked the door behind her.

Cool for a change in the hottest and driest of summers, the wind nipped my bare arms as I walked along Gas Line Road on my way to work. Puffball clouds drifted down from the north. Purple martins lined the light wires like clothespins. Noisy clouds of sparrows and blackbirds rose from their roosts as one and fanned out across the sky. Yellow showed in the hickories, red in the sumac and scarlet sage. Every August was the same. Something reassuring about that. Though, if you looked too far ahead to winter, something disquieting, too.

The phone rang when I opened my office door. "Where have you been?" was the first thing Edna Pyle said to me. The town gossip and the nearest thing to a reporter I had, Edna Pyle called me each morning to fill me in on all the small details in the life of Oakalla.

"I had a late breakfast this morning," I said. At least late for Monday, which usually found me in my office by seven.

"Fine way to run a newspaper. No wonder you can't get things right if you're never here." Like all good reporters Edna wanted to get her facts straight, and when I didn't, she was usually the first one to remind me. That was if she could beat Ruth to it.

"What didn't I get right this time, Edna?" Looking out my office window, I saw more clouds drifting down from the north.

"Just about everything," she said. "Jayne Vanderhorn spells her name with a *y*. It's not plain Jane, the way you have it. Margaret Cleaver lives at 103 Perrin Street, not 102. And the Gleaner Class party was held in the Methodist parsonage, not in the basement of the church. Punch and *cookies*, not cake, were served as refreshments. I should know. I baked them myself."

"Anything else?" I asked, noticing that the point of my pencil had started to wear down.

"An apology would be in order."

"I'm sorry, Edna. I'll try to do better next time."

"I mean for hanging up on me last Friday afternoon."

Technically I hadn't hung up on her. I'd accidentally pulled the plug out of the jack on my way to throw the phone out the window. That was after I'd called the administration building at the University of Wisconsin in Madison for information on Devin LeMay's whereabouts and been put on hold for fifteen minutes until the line went dead. Following that I'd been constantly interrupted by a series of phone calls that had little to do with anything. Then Edna called to tell me how Dianne, as in Funk, spelled her name with two *n*'s not one. How was I to know how she spelled her name? Better I screw up her first name than her last.

"Again my apologies, Edna. It won't happen again."

"See that it doesn't."

The receiver was still warm when the phone rang again. Howard Heavin, owner of Heavin's Market and one of my most faithful advertisers, said, "Garth, I see you're up and at them already."

The sun disappeared under a huge cabbage-head cloud that seemed larger than the sky itself. "Yes, Howard, up and at them."

He was apologetic. "I haven't called at a bad time, have I?"

"No, Howard. Time is not something you pay a whole lot of attention to in this business."

"Well, it's not something I like to spring on you the first thing Monday morning . . ." I waited while he found the courage to add, "But I just haven't been happy with my ads lately."

"In what way not happy?" Since he was the one who wrote his ads, I wondered if I was displaying them poorly.

"I don't know," he said. "I just don't like the way they look. Something's missing somehow."

"Is it in the lettering? We could go larger or smaller or change the type," I suggested.

"No, that's not it," he said. Then he whispered as if afraid someone might overhear. "To be honest, I don't like the way it reads. 'Get your stuffed sausage at Howard's. More meat in our links.' It makes me sound like I'm running a cathouse, not a meat market."

11

"Then why not let me write the ad?" Which I'd wanted to do for seven years. "You tell me what you want to feature and how much space you want to buy and let me do the rest."

"I don't think I can do that."

"Why not?" Though I already knew the answer.

"It's Elizabeth, you see." He lowered his voice again. "She thinks nobody can write that ad but her." Elizabeth was Howard's wife of over thirty years.

"Then what do you want me to do?"

"I don't know. I'd say that's up to you."

"Let me give it some thought, Howard."

"Thanks, Garth. I knew I could count on you."

I hung up, leaned back, and put my feet up on my desk to think about Howard Heavin's ad when my office door opened and Sheriff Rupert Roberts walked in. Tall and thin, with a somber face, bloodhound eyes, and large workman hands, he always looked pensive to me, like someone who'd just shot his horse. Our paths had often crossed, sometimes collided, during my seven years in Oakalla, but I'd never had, nor wanted, a better friend.

"I see you're hard at it," he said, taking off his hat and laying it on my desk between my feet.

"I'm thinking," I said in my defense.

"About what?"

"Howard Heavin's ad, among other things."

He stared impassively at me without betraying his thoughts. He looked fatherly. "Ruth called to say you wanted to see me," he said.

"I don't remember telling her that."

He picked up his hat, adjusted the brim, and put it back down again. He probably wanted a chew of tobacco, but since he had nowhere to spit, fought the

12

temptation. "Maybe she just assumed that," he said. "From what you told her."

"Told her about what?"

"Diana."

I sat up in my chair. "That's crazy. It's just a feeling I have. There's no reason to get you involved."

"Why not let me decide that?"

I hesitated. Involving Rupert meant admitting that there was something to worry about. Up until then I'd managed to deny that. "I don't know what I can tell you that I haven't already told Ruth," I said. "Or what you can do that I haven't already done."

His mouth crinkled, about the closest he came to a smile. "If you don't mind me asking, what have you already done?"

"Called the University of Wisconsin to check on Devin LeMay. As of last Friday, he'd already missed the week of orientation. I was getting ready to call today to see if he'd showed up for class, but I haven't had the chance."

"He hasn't," Rupert said. "I already called."

I felt the rock in my stomach shift. "No word from him at all?"

"No. Not that first one."

"That's not good news," I said.

"I wouldn't think so."

I leaned back in my chair to watch the sun finally find its way out from behind the cabbage-head cloud, only to slip behind another cloud. "See what you can do," I said.

"I plan to."

The phone rang. He picked up his hat and started for the door. "If that's Clarkie," he said, "tell him I just left."

Clarkie was Chief Deputy Harold Clark, a com-

13

puter whiz, and in Rupert's words a "real-world drop-out." Together, however, with Rupert in charge, they made a good team, and were in many ways indispensable to each other—though Rupert would never admit it, not even under oath.

I answered the phone. It was Clarkie, looking for Rupert. I told him Rupert had just left. "What was that all about?" I asked after Clarkie hung up.

"Nothing in particular. He just likes to keep track of me. I like to keep one step ahead of him."

I smiled. "And you say you don't need him."

He didn't bother to answer.

I spent the rest of the morning in my office, ate lunch at the Corner Bar and Grill, went back to work, then started home just as the blackbirds and sparrows were returning to town. I noticed that with the drought finally broken, the grass in the yards was the greenest it had been all summer—a second spring, as Sniffy Smith described it to me.

After turning the corner toward home, I crossed Diana's yard to her front porch. A deep silence answered my knock. It followed me all the way to my door.

Wearing a brown-buttoned, pea-green wool sweater and her oldest pair of brown slacks, Ruth sat at the kitchen table eating a bowl of tomato soup. Her jaw set and stubborn, her steel-gray eyes turned inward, she looked like an old sea captain moored in the eye of a storm.

"A penny for your thoughts," I said.

She ignored me.

I fixed myself a cup of instant coffee and sat down at the table across from her. "What's for supper?" I asked, because except for the soup I didn't smell anything cooking.

"Nothing yet," she answered. "But I'll come up

14

with something." She got up from the table and began banging pots and pans around, though I still didn't see any real progress toward supper.

"Rupert stopped by my office today," I said.

She stopped shuffling pots and pans long enough to say "So?"

"He said you called him."

"I did."

"You mind telling me why?"

She straightened, bringing the bean pot with her. "If you'd take a good look at yourself, you'd know why. You're not yourself, Garth. You haven't been for the past week or so."

"I could say the same for you."

"It's the heat. You know how I am in hot weather."

I knew how she was in hot weather. Wisconsin–born-and-bred, she started to wilt as soon as the temperature rose above seventy-five.

"Which is why you're wearing your sweater," I said. "Because it's so hot out."

She gave me a look that said to back off. "Why I'm wearing this sweater is no business of yours."

"That's only true as long as your business and my business have nothing to do with each other."

She turned her back to me and began pouring beans into the pot. "I'm cold, that's all," she said. "So that should be the end of it."

I took a drink of my coffee. "What aren't you telling me, Ruth? Is your chill part of the same thing that's kept you up past midnight the last few nights?"

She turned to ask, "How did you know I was up past midnight?"

"Because I couldn't sleep either."

"Yes," she admitted. "It's partly the same thing that's kept me up past midnight the past few nights."

"Which is?"

The phone rang before she had a chance to answer. "Garth, Rupert here. I've got some information on Devin LeMay, though I'm not sure how well you're going to like it."

"How bad is it?" I asked.

"Not good, considering the circumstances."

"Let me hear it anyway," I said, preparing myself for the worst.

But Rupert had his own way of delivering bad news. "Why don't we start with you," he said. "You tell me what you know about him, and that'll save us from covering the same ground twice."

What did I know about him? My heart was beating so fast it was hard to think. I knew he was a professor of English at the University of Wisconsin and had been for the past several years. He drove a silver Porsche, lived on Lake Mendota, and had published two books of poetry, which I liked better than I thought I would. The one time I met him he wore jeans, deck shoes, a shiny brass cowboy buckle on his belt, and a dark green polo shirt. He had red hair, fair skin, small bright green eyes, and looked to be in his mid-thirties. Beyond that I didn't know much else about him and told Rupert so.

"He used to live with his mother on Lake Mendota until she died a few years ago," Rupert said. "Then he married a girl named Helen Carter, who was his former student as well as his next-door neighbor there on the lake." He paused before adding, "Three years ago she disappeared and hasn't been seen since."

It took a moment to find my voice. "What do they think happened to her?"

"No one knows. The Madison police questioned Devin LeMay about it several times, but he came up clean every time. The way they figure it is that she ran away with a fellow student named John Knight. No one's seen him for the past three years either."

I noticed Ruth had moved away from the stove just far enough to hear what was going on. "Not a trace of either one of them?" I asked.

"No. Not a trace."

"What did Devin LeMay have to say about their disappearance?"

"'Heartbroken' was the way my source described him to me. Apparently he had befriended John Knight. As the story goes, Devin LeMay found him in the bush somewhere and brought him home to educate him. John Knight repaid him by running off with his wife."

Ruth edged closer until her ear was next to mine. I tilted the receiver so she could hear. "Didn't Devin LeMay have any idea where they went?" I asked.

"He didn't know. He tried to locate John Knight in the place where he found him, but John Knight wasn't there."

"Where was that?"

"I don't know. Up north somewhere."

A chill passed through me. "You're sure?"

"That's the word I got. Why?"

"Because that's where Diana went with Devin LeMay. Up north."

"What are you thinking, Garth—that there's some connection between Diana's disappearance and what I just told you?"

"Isn't that what you're thinking?"

"Yes," he admitted. "But I wanted to be sure I was on the right track." Satisfied that she'd heard enough, Ruth returned to the stove. "There's something else you ought to know," Rupert said. "Somebody else besides you is worried about Devin LeMay. She's called the

17

Madison police several times asking if they've heard anything from him."

"She give her name?"

"No."

"That's par for the course."

"I can't argue with that."

"Thanks, Rupert. Keep in touch."

"I plan to."

"Well?" I said to Ruth after I hung up. "What do you think?"

"About what?"

"Our conversation."

"I didn't hear all of it," she said, evading the question.

I filled her in.

She rested her hands on the stove. Her thoughts seemed far away, buried miles deep in the past. "I think," she said, choosing her words carefully, "that nothing's as simple as it seems."

"Do you care to explain yourself?"

She cubed some ham and threw it into the pot of beans. "When the time comes."

# 2

The first time I saw Diana she wore jeans and one of Fran's old white dress shirts and sat in her backyard sketching her apple tree. I stopped alongside the five-and-dime store to stare at her. Sitting barefoot amid apple blossoms and bluegrass on a warm spring day that fairly danced with life, she seemed out of place in Oakalla, a small Wisconsin town that might at the most have two thousand people in it. Then she saw me and waved me over to where she sat.

"What do you think?" she asked, not quite sure of herself.

It was hard to think looking into those pale gray eyes of her. "What do I think about what?" I asked.

"My sketch."

I saw it for the first time. "Not bad. Quite good actually."

She brightened. "Do you really think so?"

"Yes, I really think so." I looked at the sketch more closely. "It's the best-looking apple tree I've ever seen."

"You're just saying that," she teased. But she didn't ask me to take it back. "You're new around here, aren't you?" she continued. "At least I don't remember seeing you before."

"I'm Garth Ryland," I said, offering my hand. "I just bought the *Oakalla Reporter* a couple weeks ago."

She took my hand in hers. It felt soft and warm. At the same time I also noticed the wedding ring on her other hand. "I'm Diana Baldwin," she said. "My husband, Fran, and I grew up here."

When I let go of her hand, I was at a loss for words. It seemed I should say something meaningful or clever to help her remember me, but all I could do was to stand and stare at her like a ten-year-old kid. She said much later that she felt the same way and couldn't find the right words either. "Well," I said, finally breaking the silence. "I'd better get to work."

"Nice to have met you," she said.

"Yeah. Same here."

I didn't remember walking on to the *Oakalla Reporter* or what I did once I got there. All I remembered was my first look into her eyes and the way they smiled at me, as if they couldn't help themselves. What had she seen in me, I wondered, to call me over there to ask my opinion? And would she keep seeing it once she got to know me better? Then I reminded myself that she was married and decided that I'd be far better off to stay away from her. But I knew that I wouldn't stay away from her no matter how good it was for me. In everyone's life there's someone like that.

"Where to today?" Ruth asked as we sat at the kitchen table eating breakfast. She wore her flowered pink robe, a shawl over that, and the fur-lined moccasins I'd given her for Christmas.

"Devin LeMay's. I can't learn anything more here."

"What about the *Oakalla Reporter*?"

"It'll have to keep until I get back."

"I can baby-sit it if you like," she offered.

That surprised me because she'd never offered before. "Why?" I asked.

"Because I don't want to sit around here by myself all day."

"No other reason?" I asked.

"No other reason," she lied.

"Suit yourself," I said. "But you'll probably be bored."

"I'll take that chance."

Outside, a cool dewy morning greeted me. High up in my walnut tree, a squirrel chewed on a nut, shucking bits of shells that pattered rainlike on the leaves before falling to the ground. A robin bounced around the yard, searching hard for a late-August worm while a dog-eared tomcat, looking like he'd lost every fight in each of his nine lives, sauntered up the alley toward home.

Jessie, Grandmother Ryland's brown Chevy sedan and her last laugh on me, waited for me in the garage. In the seven years I'd owned her Jessie had put me through every test possible to see how far she could go before I killed her. It wasn't that I hadn't tried. But like the woman who once owned her, Jessie was as tough as she was contrary. I admired that in her. And save for driving her without oil, or over a cliff, both of which Ruth had recommended, I could find no good way of ridding myself of her. Trading her in on another car seemed cowardly. Selling her outright would constitute fraud. Giving her away was the ideal solution, but nobody in Oakalla was that stupid. So I kept on driving

21

her in the hope that one day she would take it upon herself to commit suicide. So far I hadn't been that lucky.

Devin LeMay lived high on the east shore of Lake Mendota in one of those solid and stately lake homes that never go out of style. Facing west across the lake, the house had been built into the hill at its back, so even though you entered the house at ground level, if you kept on walking toward the lake, you would walk out of the house on another level several feet below where you started.

Lakeside, a deck extended from a screened-in porch. A white pier and boathouse sat at the water's edge. Maple-shaded and strewn with yellow cotton-wood leaves, the yard sloped gently toward the lake in knobs and swales that reminded me of a golf course. An iron weather vane pointed southwest. A steel boy with a lantern cupped his hand to his eyes and peered out over the lake, as if watching for his absent owner.

Entering the garage, I didn't see Devin LeMay's silver Porsche, which I'd first discovered parked outside of Diana's apartment on a night I was still trying to forget. I knocked at the back door of the house, the side door, then the door to the screened-in porch. No one answered at any of them.

I took a walk to the end of the pier, stepping gingerly around a lawn chair and towel as I went. It was quiet there on the end of the pier—waves gently lapping the posts on their way to shore, dots of sailboats in the distance, a flock of snow geese preening themselves as they drifted along with the breeze. Had I been Devin LeMay, I would have lived there, too.

On my way to shore I stopped to examine the boathouse, which sat with its back to the seawall right at the water's edge. I found a ski rope, harness, and a silver-and-black slalom ski, but no boat inside on the lift. Perhaps Devin LeMay had taken it with him up north.

I saw her shadow before I saw her. She stood in the yard a few feet away, trying to identify me. Rising expectantly on her tiptoes, she was about to call out to me when something changed her mind. She settled back on her heels, disappointed. Apparently she'd mistaken me for someone else.

"Who are you?" she asked with the unquestioned right to do so.

"I might ask you the same question."

I walked out into the sunlight where she could get a good look at me and I could get a good look at her. Long and sleek with short blond hair, ice-blue eyes, and a button on the end of her nose, she wore a black one-piece swimming suit cut high on the sides, and an even coppery tan a couple shades darker than mine. She also wore a frown that deepened the longer we stood there.

"I repeat," she said evenly. "Who are you?"

"Garth Ryland. Who are you?"

As I said my name, an unmistakable look of recognition came over her. "Have we met before?" I asked, knowing that we hadn't.

"No," she answered sharply. "I've heard Dev . . . Dr. LeMay mention you a time or two."

"In class or in private?" She looked like she could have been one of his students.

She didn't answer. Turning abruptly toward the pier, she dived into the lake, swam a long leisurely lap, and returned to the pier to find me waiting for her. I offered my hand, but she brushed it aside, preferring to climb onto the pier by herself. She sat down on the edge of the pier with her back to me and dangled her feet in the water, as if hoping I'd then leave. I took her towel off her chair, draped it over her shoulders, then sat on the pier beside her.

Several minutes passed without either of us speaking. She trembled every few seconds, and her legs had goose bumps on them. But there in the sun it didn't feel that cold to me.

"Who are you, Garth Ryland?" she asked. "And why are you here?" Her eyes burned bright, yet cold, like desert stars. I couldn't read them. They could be the eyes of a poet, or an assassin, depending on her mood.

"I think you already know who I am," I said. "As for why I'm here, I'm looking for Devin LeMay."

"Why are you looking for Dev . . ." She caught herself a second time. "Dr. LeMay?"

"Why don't you just call him Devin," I said. "We're not fooling anybody here."

She gave me a look that would have frozen an Eskimo. "What do you mean by that?"

"Nothing you should take personally. It's an observation, that's all."

She glanced away, hiding whatever was in her eyes. "I've known Devin LeMay all of my life," she said. "He married my older sister." She turned back to me with the look of a precocious child who has always known she was smarter than anybody else. "He should have married *me*."

"Do you have a first name?"

"Jenny," she said, entranced by the sound. "Jenny Carter."

"And you're how old?"

"Twenty-one."

"And Devin LeMay is how old?"

She had to think on that. "Thirty-four," she said, not quite sure of herself.

24

"So you've loved him for how long?"

"Forever," she said.

"From near or afar?"

She peered into the lake. "Afar," she said dejectedly.

She pulled her legs from the water and sat with her head resting on her knees. I stared out across Lake Mendota, where the geese looked like sailboats and the sailboats looked like geese.

Then she said with more than a trace of bitterness in her voice, "But you're really not here looking for Devin. You're really here because of Diana."

"Guilty as charged," I said with a smile.

She didn't smile back. Apparently she didn't have any to spare. "She's not here," she said.

"Who isn't?"

"Diana. Neither is Devin."

"I didn't think they were. Do you know where they are?"

"No," she said. "I don't."

"Do you have any idea where they might be?"

Fear crept into her eyes, clouding them. "Yes. But I haven't told anyone."

The rock in my guts started rolling. "Where's that?"

"With John Knight." She could barely speak his name.

I felt the rock hit bone. "The same John Knight that Devin once befriended?"

"Yes," she whispered.

"I thought he was missing, along with your sister Helen."

Her eyes widened. "He *was* missing, up until a few weeks ago. Then Devin got a call from him. I was there in the house at the time." We were interrupted as a boat and a skier sliced through the morning calm. "John

25

Knight wanted Devin to come up north to visit him. He said he had a surprise for Devin."

"Did Devin have any idea what that surprise might have been?"

"He didn't say." She glanced behind her along the pier to shore, as if afraid someone might overhear. "But I think it might have had something to do with Helen."

"Your missing sister?"

"Yes," she said without emotion. "My missing sister." The skier came by again, jumping the boat's wake and throwing a rooster tail our way. "Poor Devin," she said, as if she were talking about a child. "He's such a fool where women are concerned. He's like a cocker spaniel who thinks everybody loves him the way he loves them because he's so cute and cuddly and lovable. And maybe they do love him for a while, until they get tired of him."

"Is that what happened with your sister Helen? She got tired of him?"

"Yes," she answered dully. "Just like Diana has."

"How do you know that?"

"I know, that's all. We women usually do."

"Does Devin know?"

"No," she said scornfully. "He's always the last to know about everything."

"For instance?" I said.

"John Knight and Helen," she answered. "Devin thinks, if they're together at all, they're just palling around the country, or something like that. He thinks that once Helen gets tired of that kind of life, she'll come back home to him."

"Maybe she will," I said.

"If she can."

"Meaning what?"

26

She avoided my eyes. "Nothing. Just a hunch I have."

"Which is?"

"Helen's dead."

"By John Knight's hand?" I asked.

"Yes," she said.

"Have you told Devin what you think?"

"No. He wouldn't believe me anyway. He still thinks of John Knight as his friend. He won't even admit to me that there was anything between John Knight and Helen, or that either one of them was even capable of such a thing."

"Nobody is that naive."

"Devin is," she said with certainty.

I stood up, helping her to her feet. "Let's go," I said.

"Where?" she asked.

"Do you know where in the north John Knight lives?"

"No. Up north, that's all I know."

"Then I need to take a look inside Devin's house. Do you have a key?"

She reddened. "Yes. But it belongs to my family, so we can look after Devin's house whenever he's gone."

"What will your family say if we go in there?"

"Nothing," she said. "They're on vacation in Florida. They will be until October. We have a condominium down there."

She and I exchanged glances. I didn't know what mine said, but hers said more than I needed to know. Then she started up the pier. Too aware that I was watching her every step, every twitch of her otter-sleek body, I still couldn't keep my eyes off her.

I waited for her on Devin LeMay's screened-in porch. She came back wearing a short white terry robe

27

over her black bathing suit. The robe didn't cover much. If anything, it made her look even more alluring. But maybe she knew that.

Inside, Jenny Carter went from room to room opening windows, while I took my own tour of the house. In the kitchen I found two dirty wineglasses, an empty wine bottle, a bowl of blackened bananas, a swarm of gnats, and a few drowsy flies, but not much of interest. From there I wandered down the hall into Devin Le May's study, which, like the rest of the house, had white plaster walls and black wainscoting. A black-and-white abstract painting hung on one wall. Another wall was filled with books, most of them limited editions.

*Heart of Darkness, An American Tragedy, Madame Bovary, The Brothers Karamazov, Faust, Salome,* and *Pygmalion* lined the shelves with brittle elegance. As I opened *The Turn of the Screw* by Henry James, it squeaked in protest, as if I'd violated its virgin white pages. I put it back among the others and left the study.

"What's in here?" I asked Jenny Carter on her way down the hall. I'd stopped outside a black door with a large round white knob.

"*Her* room," she said with a vengeance.

"Her room?"

"*Her* room," she repeated. "Devin's mother's room."

"I thought she was dead."

"She is."

"Then why does he keep it locked?"

"Because that's the way she wanted it."

"Do you have a key?"

She gave me a curious look. "I might be able to find one. But," she added, "Devin's very particular about that room. He won't even let me in there."

"I promise not to touch anything."

"That's not the point," she protested.

"What is the point?"

She smiled for the first time. She wanted to see inside that room as much as I did. "Nothing," she said. "I'll go get the key."

She produced a key from somewhere, and a moment later I followed her inside the room. It felt cool, tomblike, and had the thick odor of must, as do all rooms that have been kept closed for too long. Another smell—of camphor and wintergreen—had permeated the walls and the floor, even the fiber of the room itself. The room smelled and felt sick, and no amount of sunlight and fresh air would ever bring it back to health again.

"I can see why you don't like this room," I said to Jenny.

She turned on the light, which revealed a brass bed with a heavy white spread. The spread was turned back to the pillows, sheathed in pale yellow linens the color of jaundice.

"I never said I didn't like the room," Jenny answered. "I said it was *her* room."

There were no windows in the room. Someone had bricked them over. I mentioned it to Jenny.

"Devin's mother wanted it that way," she said. "She was afraid someone might come through the window after her."

"Wouldn't locks have done as well?" I asked.

"You didn't know Devin's mother," she said scornfully.

"Just as well," I said to myself.

Satisfied she'd seen enough of the room for one lifetime, Jenny left, taking the key with her. As the door started to close behind her, I reached out and threw it open again. "If you don't mind," I said to Jenny, "I don't like to be closed in."

"I don't mind," she answered. Though something in her eyes said she did.

Like the windows, the fireplace on the east wall had been bricked closed. Perhaps the late Mrs. LeMay was afraid Santa would slip down the chimney one night and mug her. On the wall above the walnut mantel hung several old photographs in glass frames that had been placed exactly so, to highlight the framed yellow document serving as a centerpiece. I stepped closer to try to read it, pausing over each word in turn, but the writing on the document had faded to the point where it was almost illegible. And when a photograph caught my eye, I happily gave up on the document and turned my attention to the photograph.

Dressed in a fluffy white gown that not even an angel would wear, a young woman, who looked about seventeen, though she must have been older, sat beside a small boy in a blue-and-white sailor suit. Standing gravely at attention, as if the weight of the world were upon his shoulders, the boy had his hand raised in a salute to something I couldn't see. Perhaps to his dead father, since his mother appeared totally helpless in the face of reality, as though she even more than her son needed someone to take care of her. I felt sorry for her. I felt sorrier for her son, who out of necessity had stepped in to be mother and father to them both.

"Who's this?" I asked Jenny, who had slipped back into the room and stood uneasily behind me.

"Devin and his mother," she answered.

"She was a pretty girl," I said, turning back to the photograph. "Do you know how old she was when this picture was taken?"

"Why don't you ask her," she said. "She's there in that vase on the mantel."

My eyes fastened on the small bronze urn that sat directly below the photograph. "Another one of her requests?" I asked.

"She said she never wanted to leave this room. Devin took her at her word."

A chill passed over me. Something in the way she said it made it seem sinister. "Did she ever leave this room?"

"Only at the last when she was starving herself to death. Devin finally had to take her to the hospital. But by then it was too late."

"Why didn't he take her sooner?" I asked.

"She wouldn't go. She said she wanted to die here. With dignity," she added for my benefit. She looked around the room, seeing more of it than I did. "Now are you about done?" she asked. "Devin wouldn't like it if he knew I let you in here."

"I'm about done," I said. "Just give me a couple more minutes."

"I'll be in the kitchen." On her way out she eyed the door, as though she wanted to close it again, but the look on my face said it wouldn't be a good idea. So she left the door open and me in peace.

Opening what I thought was a closet door, I discovered a fully furnished bathroom, complete with sink, towel, tub, and washcloth. The sink and the tub—which was narrow and deep—had white porcelain handles and shiny brass faucets. The towel and wash- cloth were lavender, Diana's favorite color, with a matching lavender bath mat. Stark and spotlessly clean, the bathroom had an elegance that Diana would have liked.

On my way out of the room, I stopped once more

31

to stare at the photograph of Devin LeMay and his mother. Something about it made me want to take it home to Ruth for safekeeping. Then I noticed the door for what appeared to be an old laundry or coal chute in the wall adjoining the hallway. Raising the metal door a few inches, the highest it would go, I peered outside to see Jenny Carter standing in the hallway, staring intently at the door where I would exit. I fought the urge to reach out and grab her by the ankle just to see what she would do. Instead I quietly lowered the door, turned out the light, and left.

As soon as the door closed, Jenny locked it, then put the key inside the pocket of her robe. "Seen enough?" she asked.

"Almost."

"What's the point of all of this anyway?" she demanded. "How's this going to help you find Devin?"

"I'm not looking for Devin," I reminded her. "I'm looking for Diana."

"They're together. You and I both know that."

"So they are," I said, hoping she'd let it go at that.

But Jenny Carter wouldn't let it go at that. "So what's the point," she repeated, "in snooping through Devin's house?"

I gave her my best answer. "Because until you've looked, you never know what you might find."

"You won't find anything here that will help you find either Devin or Diana," she assured me. "I know because I've looked."

"You're probably right," I agreed, moving on.

At the end of the hall we climbed a narrow stairs to the next floor. Following Jenny Carter step by step, so closely at times that we touched, I decided that no matter what his intentions, the best thing for a lonely heart was not a long lovely blonde who smelled like coconuts.

With mirrors on three walls, a mirror on the ceiling, a barbell, set of weights, and stationary bike on the carpet, and a zebra-striped spread and white satin pillows on his water bed, Devin LeMay's bedroom took up nearly that whole story. Like the rest of the house, it was done in contrasts, the walls white, the carpet black, the ceiling a charcoal gray that resembled a storm cloud. And Devin LeMay's room, like his mother's, had no windows to spoil his view. One narrow shaft of light came in through a skylight in the ceiling, a white shadow on the black carpet.

I stared at the bed, then the mirrors, thought of Diana, and tried to put it out of my mind.

"What's wrong?" Jenny asked.

"Nothing," I answered. "But I think I've seen enough after all."

She gave me a look that was both knowing and intimate. "So have I," she said.

We went outside and stood under the maple tree where Jessie was parked. Sadness showed on Jenny's face as she approached Jessie. She stuck her head in the window and ran her hand slowly over the steering wheel as if remembering better days. At twenty-one she seemed to have already lived one lifetime.

"What do you call her?" she asked.

"Her name is Jessie, short for Jezebel. She belonged to my grandmother Ryland. I inherited her when Grandmother died."

"Aunt Sarah's car was named Pearl," she said. "Once when we were kids, she took Helen and me to California and back in it." She smiled as she remembered. "That was the best time of my life."

33

"I think I'm living the best time of my life," I said. "Forty isn't as old as it seems at twenty."

"So Devin keeps telling me," she said without enthusiasm.

"You sound awfully old for someone so young."

She pushed away from Jessie and stood with her back to me. "That's my problem, isn't it," she said.

"Another observation," I replied. "Nothing personal."

She turned to face me. "Well, I don't like your observations."

"Sometimes neither do I."

That disarmed her. "Why don't you just leave," she said weakly. "You got what you came for."

"Which is?" I asked.

"A look inside Devin's bedroom. I know you've been dying to see it."

"One of us anyway," I said.

"I hate you," she replied, turning to leave.

"Jenny, I need a photograph of Devin. One of Helen, too, if you don't mind."

"Why should I give them to you?"

"Why shouldn't you give them to me?" I asked. "We're both on the same side, aren't we?"

She left without an answer.

Not knowing whether she'd return or not and unwilling to bet either way, I sat in the grass and shredded a leaf down to its ribs, watched a squirrel bury a walnut in the ground, and tried not to think too hard about anything. But I kept hearing something thumping above the wind. Like a distant drum that falls just within earshot, it wouldn't let my mind rest. Though when I tried to pin it down, it stopped.

Jenny returned with a single photograph that she

34

reluctantly handed to me. "It's my neck if you lose this," she said. "So whatever you do, be careful with it."

Taken lakeside in Devin LeMay's yard, framed by spring maples with blue waves as a backdrop, the photograph was of Helen Carter and Devin LeMay on their wedding day. Never had I seen a happier groom. His unbounded childlike joy, that pure joy of being, was that of a climber on top of his first mountain, and left no question where he stood.

Helen's joy, however, was tempered, less complete, as if her happiness needed to be measured for fear of running out one day. In her I saw the same reticence—though not the same estrangement—as on the face of Devin LeMay's mother: the same look of someone awed by life's demands rather than its grandeur. Perhaps her fears were justified and she already knew that in the end life would prove too much for her.

Glancing from the photograph of Helen to the face of Jenny Carter, I saw the family resemblance. But Helen was a fragile beauty who appealed to one's manhood as her hunter-protector, while Jenny was cool and sublime, and, like a sleek jungle cat, evoked intrigue and danger and stirred the juices of conquest. Of the two I didn't know which I preferred. One might consume, the other castrate you.

"Your sister is very beautiful," I said to Jenny.

"Beauty is as beauty does," she answered.

"But no more beautiful than you."

"Beauty is as beauty does," she repeated.

I didn't need to hear it a third time. "When did Devin think he'd be home?" I asked.

"He didn't know exactly. Just that he'd be home in time for orientation."

"Which started a week ago yesterday."

"And ended last Friday."

"And classes started yesterday?" I asked.

"Yes," she answered.

"Then why aren't you in class?"

The question surprised her. She also seemed to resent it. "I'm supposed to be. But with Devin missing I can't get interested."

"Would Devin approve of your cutting classes?"

"I don't care whether he approves or not. Devin LeMay isn't my father. Though sometimes he acts like it."

"But you are the one who's been calling the Madison police, asking about him."

"How did you know that?"

I tapped my forehead. "Kidneys."

"I want a straight answer. How did you know that?"

I stood, preparing to leave. "John Knight," I said. "What all can you tell me about him?"

"Are you going to answer my question?"

"I know you've been calling the Madison police because somebody has, and it stands to reason you're the one. Nobody's tapped your phone, if that's what you're worried about."

Her look said she didn't quite believe me.

"John Knight," I repeated. "What can you tell me about him?"

"Not much," she said sullenly. "I only met him a couple times when Devin had him over to his house."

"Did he make any impression on you?"

"Not any good impression. I've seen his type before."

"Meaning what?"

"Meaning John Knight wasn't quite as dumb as he made everybody think he was, or as backward."

"Do you think he was putting on an act?"

36

"Yes." She left no room for doubt.

"For whose benefit?"

"Devin's, of course. He's the one who brought John Knight here."

"At whose insistence?"

She smiled. "You catch on fast, don't you?"

"Helen's, right? She's the one who really brought John Knight here."

She didn't answer.

"Which was it, Jenny?" I asked. "Devin or Helen?"

"Helen," she said. "Though she made it seem like it was Devin's idea." Her face hardened, like that of a child twice betrayed. "There's something else you might want to know, something I haven't told anyone before, not even Devin. The night before Helen and John Knight disappeared I saw her talking to him out by the pier while Devin was asleep. Then she came into our house to pack a suitcase with some of her old clothes, which she'd left in her room at home."

"Did she take the suitcase with her?"

"Yes. At least it was gone the next day when I came home from class."

"Why didn't you tell Devin about it?"

"Because he wouldn't have believed me," she said. "He never has where Helen's concerned."

I got into Jessie. Before closing the door, I asked, "Is there anyone at the university who might know John Knight's whereabouts?"

She thought a moment, then said, "Ned Emery. You might ask him."

"Who's Ned Emery?"

"A friend of Devin's. He teaches poetry, I think."

"What makes you think he might know where John Knight is?"

"I'm not sure he does. But he would if anyone does."

"Thanks. I'll look him up."

I began to back slowly out of the drive. Jenny Carter walked up the drive beside me. "You won't be coming back here again, will you?" she asked.

"You never know," I answered. "Why?"

"No reason, I guess," she said, sounding disappointed.

I left, waving as I turned onto the road and away from the lake. She might have waved back, but I didn't see her.

# 3

I ate lunch at the Rathskellar in the Union Building, then spent the next couple hours wandering the campus while waiting for Ned Emery to return to his office from class. The feeling of the campus really hadn't changed much in the twenty-one years I'd been gone. Only the faces had changed, those of the people and the buildings themselves. The same energy was closely packed into a few city blocks along State Street; the same cool winds blew off Lake Mendota; the same late-August enclaves of students and professors gathered around their favorite watering holes in anticipation of the year ahead. Spring would find a different campus, one leaner, wiser, less in love with itself. But fall, with all its fat and frolic, was still my favorite time to be there.

Ned Emery unlocked his office door and went inside, leaving the door open. A tall man with thin brown hair, narrow shoulders, and a wide, round face, he wore tan slacks, a light green sweater over his brown shirt and tie, and the look of someone who might forget his own birthday, but never the tear in his wife's eye the night he proposed. Filled with books, plants, and photographs of his family, his office felt warm and friendly to me, like my own office back in Oakalla.

"Dr. Emery?"

He glanced at me over the top of his glasses. Until the moment I spoke, he wasn't aware that there was anyone else in the room. "Yes, what is it?"

"I'm Garth Ryland," I said. "I'm looking for Devin LeMay."

He shook my hand and returned to his notes. "Aren't we all looking for Devin LeMay," he said. "I'm teaching one of his survey courses in American literature and don't have the faintest idea of what I'm doing." After flipping through a stack of papers, he took off his glasses and rubbed his eyes in exasperation. "So, when you do find Devin, please give the bastard my regards." He leaned back, putting his glasses on.

"How about John Knight?" I said. "Should I ask him?"

"John Knight? Who in the hell is that?"

"Devin LeMay found him in the backwoods somewhere and brought him here for an education."

Ned Emery smiled. It was a closed smile, not intended to be shared. "Of course, the bearded one," he said. "According to Devin, he was the next Thoreau. I'm not sure who was fooling whom."

"I take it you weren't impressed."

"Not so," he corrected me. "John Knight was quite impressive in his beard and buckskin. He wore like an old and favored pair of slippers. Went down like fine wine. Sang your praises until even you believed him.

**40**

John Knight was the ultimate guest." He pulled a piece of notepaper from his drawer and jotted something down on it. "And bullshitter."

"A reminder to yourself?" I asked, recalling that I, too, made notes to myself.

Ned Emery smiled at me. "I'm supposed to pick up eggs and milk on the way home. I've forgotten the past two days."

"I thought you might have been recalling a line of poetry."

"As a matter of fact I was. 'I've eaten the plums you were probably saving for supper. Forgive me. They were delicious, so sweet and so cold.'" Then he looked down in embarrassment, shuffling through his notes. "Or something like that." He continued to talk as he shuffled. "It used to be I enjoyed this part of my life. Lately it's grown a little thin." He looked at me over the top of his glasses. "Never buy a farm, Ryland. It'll end up owning you."

"It's too late," I said. "I already own one."

He shook his head in sympathy. "God help you, then." Nodding toward a padded metal chair, he said, "You may as well sit down. This might take a while."

I sat in the chair while he sorted his papers and stuffed them into his briefcase. He pulled a couple of books from the shelves and also put these into his briefcase. Satisfied that he had all he needed, he set the briefcase aside, closed his office door, and leaned back with his hands clasped behind his head and his feet on his desk. I guessed that in a few years, maybe sooner than even he knew, Ned Emery wouldn't be coming into the office at all.

"What else was John Knight besides a bullshitter?" I asked.

"A ladies' man," he answered. "Or at least he tried

41

to be. I guess he was good enough at it to fool some of them."

"Like Helen Carter LeMay?"

He leaned forward to pick up a pen from his desk and put it away. "I've heard rumors, that's all."

"Then it was no surprise when she and John Knight disappeared one spring day?"

"That depends on who you ask. It surprised the hell out of Devin."

"He had no idea what might be going on between them?" I asked.

"Not in the least."

"I find that hard to believe."

"That's because you don't know Devin LeMay like I do," he said with a bemused smile. Then he stood and picked up his briefcase. "Come on, Ryland. I want to show you something. You have a car, I take it?"

"Of sorts."

"So do I, of sorts. In case we get separated, I'll meet you at the Shell station at the junction of Fifty-One and I-Ninety-Four."

"Are we going to your farm?"

"It's on the way to my farm." His face darkened. "But no, we're going somewhere else."

Three wrong turns later I met him at the Shell station, then followed his blue Volkswagen Rabbit across country in the general direction of Oakalla. As the road narrowed and the trees began to crowd the pavement, I thought I knew where we might be headed. When we approached Lost Road and he signaled to turn, I knew that I'd been right.

Partially hidden by a giant white oak that had spread out instead of up, goiterlike burls growing from its short thick limbs, the house glared at me through two wide windows, cold and opaque like the eyes of a mantis. Colorless, the face of the house rose to a sharp peak, then lost its clear lines and became something else, then something else again before it reached the ground, as if the builder, unable to decide what he wanted, cobbled in whatever next came to mind. I felt repelled by it. If a house could be such a thing, that house was evil.

"What do you think?" Ned Emery asked.

"I think I don't like it."

"I never did either."

"Then why did you bring me here?"

"You said you were looking for John Knight. Well, this is where he lived while he was on campus."

Though sunset was at least three hours away, shadows already covered every square foot of the house. "Why here?" I asked.

"You'll have to ask John Knight that. My guess is that it suited him."

"How did you know where it was?"

"John Knight threw a party. I was invited."

"Did John Knight throw many parties?"

"More than you'd think . . . for a backwoodsman," he added.

"Was John Knight a backwoodsman?" I asked.

"He had all the skills," Ned Emery answered. "But I think by necessity rather than design."

"Do you think he was on the run from something when Devin happened upon him?"

His eyes fastened on the house. "That thought has occurred to me more than once."

"Devin's supposed to be staying with John Knight," I said. "Do you have any idea where that might be?"

"I did once," he answered. "But I've forgotten." He scratched his head. "I wish now I could remember

43

because something happened this spring that's bothered me ever since. I got a long-distance call from a fur buyer who said John Knight had given him my number, with instructions to call her if the fur prices went up. The prices had gone up. The problem was, I didn't know what the hell she was talking about."

"You're sure she mentioned John Knight specifically?"

"I wasn't until you mentioned his name again today. But I am now."

"Is there a chance that John Knight planned on paying you a visit?"

"There's always that chance. But if so, he never showed up at my door."

"Were you and John Knight friends while he was here?"

He reached into his pocket to pull out his keys. "I found him entertaining," he answered. "He could tell a story with the best of them."

"Then is there any particular reason why he would suddenly decide to look you up after a three-year absence?"

"None that I can think of," he answered. "Unless he needed money."

"Did you ever offer him any?"

Ned Emery smiled. The joke was on him. "I might have, at one of my weaker intoxicated moments. I've offered a lot of things under those conditions. Fortunately, no one has taken me up on them." His smile vanished. "You feel it, too, don't you?" he said.

"Feel what?"

"This place. You feel the oppression of it. Up until now I thought I was the only one."

"I'm not sure oppression is the right word," I said. "But I feel something . . . that makes my skin crawl."

He got into his Rabbit. "Good luck finding Devin, for whatever your reason."

"I'm not looking for Devin, but someone who should be with him."

"Diana?"

I smiled at his perception. "How did you know?"

"I've met her. If I were you, I'd be looking, too."

"Thanks for your help," I said. "And don't forget the milk and eggs."

He snapped his fingers. "I knew there was something."

After turning the Rabbit around in the road, he left the way we'd come. I stood staring at the house, trying to decide whether I wanted to go in there or not. Finally I decided I didn't, at least not so late in the day.

Ruth had already started supper when I arrived home. With hamburger and onions browning in the Dutch oven and tomatoes and peppers on the cutting board, it was a good bet we were having chili. "So how did things go at the office today?" I asked while fixing myself a highball.

Ruth noticed my taking a pull on the bourbon bottle before putting it back into Grandmother Ryland's kitchen cabinet. "Maybe I should be the one doing the asking," she said.

"I saw a house today I didn't like," I answered. "It gave me a chill. Something that's been going around lately."

She ignored me and continued cutting tomatoes.

"You didn't answer my question," I said. "How did things go at the office today?"

"To use your favorite expression, they went," she replied. "But if Edna Pyle had called one more time to tell me all she knew, you'd be looking for a new stool pigeon." She turned the hamburger and onions. "I swear, I wonder what that woman does all day besides go to meetings and talk on the telephone."

"Maybe she's lonely."

"Who isn't at her age? If she'd mind her own business once in a while, maybe she'd find something to do, instead of nit picking the lint off turnips. Who cares? That's what I want to know. Who cares if the Merry Sunshine Club were served crab cakes and stuffed flounder at their luncheon?" She went back to cutting tomatoes, slicing into the board as she did. "Now, if they all got ptomaine and died, that might be news."

"Somebody cares about those details," I said, "or they wouldn't buy the paper."

"Not as much as you might think," she replied. "Give me a week with that paper and you'd see some changes made."

I called her bluff. "You might get your chance."

"Meaning what?"

"Nothing. Just a thought I had." Then I said, "What do you know about the house on Lost Road?"

She stopped cutting the tomatoes. "There aren't any houses along Lost Road. There haven't been in over eighty years. That's why they call it Lost Road."

"Well, there's one there now."

"Where?" She'd momentarily forgotten the chili.

"I don't know exactly. It's by a big gnarled white oak tree."

The knife fell from her hand, bouncing off the counter on its way to the floor. Since she made no move to retrieve it, I retrieved it for her. "Here," I said. "You dropped this."

"It can't be," she said quietly to herself.

"What can't?"

"Nothing," she said, regaining her composure. "Now get out of here so I can finish supper."

"Where do you suggest I go?"

Much to her relief, the phone rang. "You might start there."

"Garth, it's Rupert. You have any luck today?"

"Some," I said. "I think John Knight figures more in this than I'd like for him to." I told him what I'd learned.

"I agree," he said. "I made some more phone calls today . . ."

"And?" I asked when he didn't continue.

"Do you remember the rapes they had there in Madison three and four years ago? Most of them were college girls. Well, John Knight is still the chief suspect in the case."

I looked at Ruth, who had put down the knife and was listening closely. "Go on," I said.

"That's it," he replied. "When John Knight disappeared, the rapes stopped. There haven't been any to speak of since."

"Why can't you ever call with good news?"

"If I wanted to be in that business, I'd have never run for sheriff in the first place."

Ruth went back to her cooking. I went back to my highball. Each locked in his own thoughts, neither of us said much during supper.

After supper I walked to the *Oakalla Reporter*. I knew Ruth too well to think that she'd spent the day there just to keep it company. In times past I almost had to bind and gag her just to get her inside the door. Starting in my office, where I found the phone off the hook, which explained why Edna Pyle had never called Ruth back, I took a tour of the place to see what I might find. When I got to the morgue and discovered one of the drawers open, I thought I'd struck pay dirt. Instead

47

I found a note from Ruth that said, "You're wasting your time." I smiled in spite of myself.

Hours later I walked home under a crystalline sky too dense for words, like those rare thoughts that bowl you over with their purity and compromise all the thoughts you've had before. It wasn't until I reached my back door that I realized in all of my goings and comings that day, I hadn't stopped by Diana's once.

# 4

"*I*'m not going with you," Ruth said. "When I left there, it was for good. I haven't been on Lost Road since." Ruth and I sat at the kitchen table with the remains of breakfast in front of us. A south breeze blew in the kitchen window, smelling like walnuts and marigolds.

"I need a guide, Ruth. I don't know that area like you do."

She took a drink of coffee and set the cup down again. "What's the good in going there? You already said the house was deserted. What do you think you'll find?"

"I don't know. But don't you find it strange that after eighty years there's a house on Lost Road, and that house just happened to be where John Knight lived?"

She wavered slightly. "Yes, it's strange. I'll grant you that. But what does it prove?"

**49**

"Nothing. But I know how I felt when I first saw it. I'd like to have your reaction."

"Why?"

"Because you're more in touch than I am."

She eyed me suspiciously. "In touch with what?"

"Feelings. Vibrations, as Diana calls them. You've said in the past you've had dreams that turned out to be true."

She avoided my eyes. "What of it," she said. "Lots of people can say that."

"But I don't know very many of them," I persisted. "And none of them I do know used to live in the Lost Road neighborhood."

"Only until I was eighteen," she argued.

"That's all of childhood." Seeing my chance, I added, "What can it hurt, Ruth? You've always said you never left anything there you wanted to go back for."

"That's the whole point, isn't it?" she said.

"Please, Ruth. I need your help."

She softened, but not much. "On one condition. When I say it's time to leave, we leave."

"Fair enough."

"And we take my car. I'm not taking the chance of having that rattletrap of yours break down on us."

Therefore, Ruth drove while I admired the islands of purple thistles that stood amid the goldenrod in the pastures and meadows, and the black-eyed Susans that lined the roadways and meandered along the creek banks. Blotches of yellow showed in the tops of some of the trees, and occasional clusters of orange maple leaves previewed the fall to come. And everywhere, among the hollows and valleys, by woodsides and watersides, lay a deep shoe-soaking dew.

So named because it led nowhere and ended in a pine thicket, Lost Road had a reputation, going back as far as I could remember, of being haunted. During the years I'd been in Oakalla, first at Grandmother Ryland's farm and then as editor of the *Oakalla Reporter*, I'd only traveled to the far end of Lost Road once, and that was enough for me. One step off of Lost Road and you plunged neck-deep into nettles and briers. If you were fool enough to keep on going, as I had on that occasion, you soon wished you hadn't. With my arms afire and my cheek laid open by a greenbrier, I'd crawled back in defeat the way I'd come, gathered my courage, and tried and tried again. When I finally broke into a clearing somewhere near the heart of the surrounding woods and discovered nothing that made the trip worthwhile, I realized that some areas were better left to themselves. Lost Road was one of them.

We stopped in front of John Knight's house. I had hoped it would look better in the morning light. It looked the way I remembered it, cold, opaque, and somehow sinister.

"I'm not going in," Ruth said. The set of her jaw left no doubt.

"I'm not asking you to."

"If you had any sense, you wouldn't go in there either," she warned.

"I can't argue with that."

Sticktights, sandburs, cockleburs, and horseweeds had taken over the front yard, while the few remaining clumps of ryegrass and bluegrass had paled in the thin sandy soil, sticking strawlike through the weeds surrounding them. Stopping beneath the giant white oak that shaded the house and most of the yard, I noticed an old lightning scar on its trunk where the bark had been ripped away and a jagged furrow burned into the trunk itself. That might explain why the trees limbs were so thick and dwarflike, and why it had grown out instead of up. Whatever the reason for its deformity, it looked as though it belonged there.

Opening the door to the house, I entered a mis-shapen room, low on one side and high on the other, and finished with a dull orange paneling that reminded me of a carnival. A fuzzy green chair and couch sat along one wall. A square brown plastic lamp hung overhead. Along the wall opposite me a wood stove and stovepipe fed into a blackened chimney, and they all looked decades older than they were. I examined the chimney. With its bricks crumbling, and chinks showing in its mortar, it had survived at least one fire in its lifetime. I guessed it was at least as old as the oak outside.

I followed the cord of the lamp to an extension cord that led to an old gasoline generator sitting on some boards just outside the back door. Another cord led from the generator into the kitchen, equipped with a gas stove and a gas refrigerator, and a yellow Formica-topped table with two yellow-padded chairs to match.

The two chairs faced each other across the table. A plate, silverware, glass, and napkin were set in place in front of each chair. A bouquet of dried flowers stood in a white vase between the two settings, dust petals heaped on the table beneath them.

A spider had built, from the vase to the black plastic lamp hung over the table, an intricate web that burned eerily in a ray of sunlight filtering through a crack in the wall. Buffeted by a sudden breeze from outside, the web began to sway, and its golden traces sawed back and forth until it seemed it would surely fall. But somehow it held fast until the breeze died, and then all returned to stillness, as before.

I smelled something rancid—perhaps a dead mouse. Opening the cabinet above the sink, I found a couple of rows of canned goods, but no mouse. Blowing the dust from one of the cans, I put it back in place.

The smell followed me into John Knight's bedroom, where two sleeping bags lay zipped together atop a mattress on the floor. Save for a single shadeless lamp and a small electric space heater that on its best days wouldn't warm a dinner roll, the mattress and sleeping bags were the only furnishings in the room. Keeping them company, off in one corner by itself, a small leather suitcase displayed the letters H.C.L. Helen Carter LeMay had gotten that far at least.

Like the living room and kitchen, the bedroom had a soft wooden floor that bounced with each step, reminding me of the boards in Grandmother Ryland's smokehouse. Except—unlike Grandmother Ryland's smokehouse—the bedroom didn't have a cellar underneath it. I didn't find one anyway when I went outside to look.

Shaded by small cedars and scrub oak, overgrown with crabgrass and sandburs, the small cemetery behind the house had a few white weathered stones, multiflora rose crowding its borders, and the look of abandonment. Long, low sandy mounds snaked their way between the stones and throughout the cemetery like huge mole runs, making it hard to walk without climbing over one. I wondered where the mounds had come from. As far as I knew, no mound builders had ever lived in the Oakalla area.

"How am I supposed to know where the mounds came from?" Ruth said in answer to my question. "They weren't there when I was a girl."

"You're sure?"

"Yes. I'm sure."

"What about the cemetery?"

"It's always been there. It's the McCorkle family

53

cemetery. Now are you ready to go?" She started the Volkswagen. "Because I am."

"Almost. If you can tell me why the name McCorkle sounds so familiar to me."

She glared at me. "Are you forgetting our agreement?"

"Ruth, it's important. When you said McCorkle, the name jumped out at me. I'd like to know why."

"And I can't tell you why." She turned the Volkswagen around in the middle of Lost Road and headed back the other way.

"You haven't been much help at all," I said in anger.

She bristled. "Meaning what?"

"Meaning just that. I'm trying my damnedest to find Diana, and you have some idea of where she is, but you won't tell me. Why don't you tell me? That's what I'd like to know."

She gave me her you-asked-for-it look. "She's in a basement."

"Where?"

"I don't know. That's where I see her."

"Why didn't you tell me that a week ago?"

"Because even if I had told you, it wouldn't help you find her."

"Why not let me decide that," I said. "Just because you don't like Diana doesn't mean you have to let her rot away somewhere."

She stopped the Volkswagen in the middle of Lost Road. "Let's get one thing straight," she said. "I never said I didn't like Diana. I do. I said I don't think she does right by you. Which she doesn't. But that's beside the point. As far as where she is, I don't have the faintest idea. It could be Oakalla, or the middle of Timbuktu. I don't know."

"But she is in a basement?"

"That's where I see her. Yes."

"Alive or dead?" I had to ask.

She didn't answer. Her thoughts were somewhere else.

"Ruth?"

She shook her head. "I honestly don't know, Garth." She gave me a rare smile, one that said that she knew what I was going through. "But, and try not to take this too hard, when it's all said and done, she's already lost to you anyway, whether you find her alive or not."

I didn't say anything.

"Pouting won't help any either," she said.

"I'm not pouting."

"Then what are you doing?"

"Thinking about where I heard the name McCorkle lately."

"Is that all?" she persisted.

"I'm also thinking about Diana and me, and what you said about us. That even if I do find her alive, she's lost to me anyway. I think I know that," I admitted. "In my head. But not in my heart."

She didn't answer.

"Is that crazy?" I asked.

"No. It's not crazy," she replied. "I felt the same when Karl died. Part of me knew he was gone for good, that nothing I could do would ever change that. Another part of me expected to walk into the living room one day and find him there asleep in his favorite chair." She rolled down her window to let some air in. "Even though you know better, you never quite give up hope."

We rode in silence to Ruth's old home place where we turned around in the drive and started back the

55

other way. All that was left of it were the foundations of the house and barn, a small tile silo that looked like new, one of the concrete posts that used to mark the drive, and a row of red pines planted as a windbreak along the north side of the house. Time, weather, and weeds had claimed the rest of it.

"You'd never know to look at it now," Ruth said sadly. "But that was once a showplace. Pop would turn over in his grave if he could see what happened to it."

"I always thought you were poor," I said, remembering the tales of her and Karl's struggles.

"Karl and I *were* poor," she said. "But I wasn't poor until I married him."

"Your dad didn't help you out?"

She shook her head, recalling the pain as if it were yesterday. "No. He didn't help us out. Mama did with her butter-and-egg money, but he never knew about it."

"Why wouldn't he help you out?"

"Because he couldn't stand the thought of his firstborn and favorite daughter marrying a farmer. He had other plans for me."

"Such as?"

"College for one. Pop had his heart set on me being a doctor. He said I'd waste my life doing anything else."

"How right was he?" I asked.

"About what?"

"Your being a doctor?"

"I'd thought about it," she admitted. "I even went so far as to put my application in at the University of Wisconsin. They even went so far as to accept me."

"What changed your mind?"

"Karl for one. I figured by the time I got out of school somebody else would have snapped him up." Her eyes clouded momentarily, then cleared again. "And there were other reasons, ones I'd just as soon not go into, why I wanted to get away from here and be done with it."

"Do you regret not going to school and being a doctor?" I said.

She took her time in answering. "I'd have made a good one," she mused. "And I was smart enough and tough enough to pull it off. But no, I have no regrets. Besides, I'd be a fool to bring them up now if I did."

We came to a farm littered with rusty farm machinery. A coon dog bayed at us from atop his box as we turned in the gravel drive, and a couple of beagle pups, along with a long-haired orange cat, ran out to greet us, scattering chickens in all directions. The cat and pups, delighted at the prospect of company, wouldn't let me take a step without petting one of them. The coon dog meanwhile howled in protest.

A short round man wearing bib overalls, a soiled John Deere cap, and a two-day growth of beard crawled out from under his combine. Jimmy Scaggs could fix anything, but never keep it running for long, which explained why his farm always resembled a junkyard. But Jimmy had a lot of heart and he could outwork, out whistle, and out neighbor almost anyone in and around Oakalla.

"Morning, Jimmy," I said.

"Morning, Garth," he answered, grease dripping down his nose. "What can I do you for?"

"I was wondering if you know who built that house along Lost Road."

We shook hands, as was our custom, and his hard, earthy grip felt good to me. "You know I've been wondering about that myself," he said. "One day I drove by and there was nothing. The next day I drove by, there the house was with someone living in it."

"When was that; do you remember?"

57

He used his shirt sleeve to wipe the grease from his nose. "A couple three summers ago, maybe longer. I had corn planted in that one field there near the end of Lost Road. The house went up between the last time I cultivated it and harvesttime."

"Which would be?"

Picking up one of the beagle pups, he scratched its ears, then set it down again. "Between July and October, sometime in there."

"You say you saw the man who was living there," I said.

"Saw him, met him, shook his hand. He was a friendly enough fellow. Told me to stop by anytime I took the notion. There'd likely be a party going on."

"Did you take him up on it?"

Jimmy smiled at me. I liked his smile. It was wide open, hiding nothing. "No. Not that I didn't think about it, especially when I saw all those college gals running around there with next to nothing on. But I doubted if Delores would have approved." Delores was Jimmy's second wife, and according to him and her both, his last one.

"What did the man look like; do you remember?" I asked.

Jimmy reached down to scratch his cat's chin and retie his shoelace, which one of the pups had untied for him. "He had a beard, a black one, if I remember right. And he drove a black pickup. One of those jacked-up jobs with the short bed on it that aren't worth a damn for nothing, except looking good." He smiled at me. "Which was sort of my impression of the man who owned it."

"Do you remember when he left there?"

He took off his cap to wipe the sweat from his brow. "Nope. He left sometime in the spring between the time I first broke ground and planted. Here today and gone tomorrow, just like he came."

"Didn't that surprise you?"

"Why should it? It was no hair off my nose."

"Don't you own the ground where he built?"

He gently nudged the pups away from underfoot. Already they had his shoe untied again and were working on the other one. "Nope. That three acres there where the house and cemetery is belongs to somebody else. All the rest there along both sides of Lost Road is mine, though."

"Do you have any idea who does own that three acres?" I asked.

Shaking his head, he knelt to tie his shoe, then crawled back under the combine. "Nope. Wish I did, though. I'd pay them to let me burn that house down."

"It's an eyesore, isn't it," I said.

"Call it what you like," he said, picking up his wrench. "It flat out gives me the creeps."

"One last question, Jimmy. Do you have any idea where those mounds in the McCorkle cemetery came from?"

He put the wrench on a nut and began loosening it. "Nope. I didn't know there were any."

"Thanks, Jimmy."

"Any time, Garth. You know you're always welcome here."

I walked back to the Volkswagen with both pups tugging at my cuffs. "He doesn't own the three acres where the house and cemetery are," I said to Ruth.

"I heard," she answered.

"Do you have any idea who does?"

"No. But Aunt Emma might."

Remembering that Diana's house had a basement and that I had a key to the house, I stopped by there on my way to Aunt Emma's after leaving Ruth and the Volkswagen off at home. As I stepped inside, the house greeted me, its scent warm and familiar. I loved that house. I loved its walls, floors, attic, and basement. I loved its history, which preceded even the town of Oakalla, and its memories. I loved to hear its grandfather clock toll the hours. I loved to lie on the floor in front of its fireplace—warm, assured, and at peace with life. But most of all I loved its owner. Without her there its heart was missing.

When I didn't find Diana in the basement, I went through the rest of the house room by room, but didn't find her there either. Leaving, I raised her garage door and was surprised to find both her 1937 Bentley and her M.G.B. That meant she and Devin had stopped in Oakalla on their way up north. Somehow that hurt even more.

Aunt Emma lived about a block north of the *Oakalla Reporter* in a two-story frame house overgrown on all sides with trees, evergreens, and bushes that had had their own way for years. Painted a dusky red with blue trim, Aunt Emma's house was piled attic to basement with mementos from all over the world, especially the Far East, where she'd served as an army nurse during World War II and after. But as she'd once confided to me during a bout with jaundice when she was convinced she was dying, her most valued treasure was a brass cartridge with the initials R.K.G. scratched on it. Had I known its history, I might have unlocked the secret of Aunt Emma, and why, though she had had dozens of offers, she had never married.

"You won't find me in there," Aunt Emma said from her side yard after I'd knocked twice on her door.

"Where will I find you, then?"

"Hard to say," she replied. "So early in the day." Dressed in her beekeeping garb, complete with gloves and goggles, she looked like the Red Baron standing there.

"Going dancing?" I asked.

"I wish," she answered.

I sat on her front step. She lit a Camel and sat beside me. Ruth and I had both given up trying to get her to quit smoking. As Aunt Emma said, she'd lived that long without our help.

"What are you up to today?" I asked.

"Collecting honey. What does it look like?"

"I didn't think there would be any because of the drought."

"More than you'd think," she said. "I've already taken off four full supers, and I'm just getting started."

"What do the bees think about that?"

She gave me a caustic look. "I'm old, Garth, not senile. The bees *don't* think about that, just like a lot of people I know. They're only plugged into direct current."

"Sorry I asked."

"You should be. We're both too old to waste any time on stupid questions." She took a drag on her Camel, as the smoke leaked slowly from her nose. "So get on with whatever you came for." Then she said with a barb in her voice, "And yes, I'm sober, so you don't have to worry about that."

"I wasn't worried about that," I said.

She gave me a smile that said I was forgiven. "I figured not."

"Ruth and I took a drive out to Lost Road today," I began. "Did you know there was a house on it?"

"No. But it's been at least twenty years since I've been out that way, so they could have put up a circus

61

there, and I wouldn't have known about it." She took another drag on her Camel. "Where is the house anyway?"

"Right in front of the old cemetery."

"Where McCorkle Chapel used to be?" she asked.

"I don't know. What was McCorkle Chapel?"

"A country church where I used to go as a young woman. So did Ruth as a kid, though I can't say it did either of us much good. It burned down during a thunderstorm one hot summer afternoon. Ruth can tell you about it. She was still living at home at the time."

"It's McCorkle Cemetery, too," I said. "Isn't it?"

Using the stub of her first cigarette, Aunt Emma lit another one. "Yes," she said. "Old Simon McCorkle had the chapel built in the hopes of saving his soul. But he was beating a dead horse. He could have built a cathedral, and his soul still would have been up for grabs."

"How so?"

Her eyes snapped as she spoke. "The man was just plain mean, Garth. There's no other word for it. And he deserved what he got."

"Which was?"

She took a long drag on her second Camel. "I'll have to fill you in first."

"I'm not sure I have that much time," I said, glancing at my watch.

"I'll keep it brief. For starters Simon McCorkle burned down his own house and nearly everyone in it, except for his young stepmother whom he later married and had children by. Who he treated like dogs, or worse, until he drove his wife crazy and all his children away from home." She paused, momentarily forgetting her cigarette. "I guess one of his children did come back

62

to live with him again, until the day she found him hanging on a hay hook in his barn, murdered by person or persons unknown." She put the Camel to her mouth, but didn't smoke it. "Ask Ruth. She can fill you in on all the details."

"I plan to. Thanks, Aunt Emma." At the end of her walk I turned back to her. "I almost forgot. Do you know who owns that piece of property where McCorkle Chapel used to be?"

"I suppose the McCorkle heirs. Once the church burned down, unless it was rebuilt, I assume the property went back to them. That's the way they usually did it in those days."

"Who might the McCorkle heirs be?"

"You'll have to ask Ruth that question. She used to be in tight with Simon's oldest daughter, the one, if I'm right on it, who left home, came back, and found him hanging in the barn. As for his other two children, I don't know what happened to them. A boy and a girl; I remember that much. And there's a mystery surrounding one of them, but I don't know which."

"Thanks again, Aunt Emma. You've been a big help."

She rose from the step, pulled down her goggles, and lit another cigarette. "Save your sweet talk for Ruth. You'll need it."

"Just what are you saying, Aunt Emma?"

"Just what I said. If you can get Ruth to talk about Esther McCorkle, you're a better man than I."

"Esther McCorkle?"

"Simon's oldest daughter. I just remembered her name."

I spent the afternoon and evening in my office. Friday's edition of the *Oakalla Reporter* would run six pages, including my weekly column and Willard Coates's article on the ins and outs of ginseng hunting. I still had my column to write, I still had to figure out Howard Heavin's ad, and I still had three pages left to fill, but I spent most of my time thinking about Diana.

The phone rang. Looking at my watch for the first time in hours, I saw that it was nearly midnight. "Don't you ever sleep?" Rupert asked.

"I might ask you the same thing." The scent of fresh-cut grass drifted in my window. I leaned back to smell it. "What do you have for me?" I asked.

"Nothing," he answered. "No one has anything on the John Knight in question."

"Maybe that's not his real name," I suggested.

"I thought of that. Which is why the first thing tomorrow I'll have Clarkie draw up a profile on that computer of his. We'll see if we can't locate him that way."

I yawned. "How long will that take?"

"Four days or four years, depending on how lucky we are."

"We don't have that long, Rupert."

"I know that," he said sharply. "But that's the best I can do for now."

"Sorry," I said.

"Accepted."

"Ruth says Diana's in a basement somewhere."

"I know," he said. "She told me that when I called. She also wondered when you were coming home."

"Soon," I answered.

"Don't wear yourself too thin, Garth. We might be looking at the long haul here."

"I'm trying not to think too hard about that." The cut grass scent grew stronger. I no longer had to put my nose to the screen to smell it.

"Something you should consider anyway. Good night, Garth."

"Good night, Rupert."

Soon turned out to be several hours later.

# 5

*I* awakened to the smell of coffee perking and bacon frying. It seemed I'd slept forever, but when I looked at my watch, it turned out to be closer to four hours. Downstairs Ruth stood over the stove with a spatula in one hand and a cup of coffee in the other. She appeared to guard the stove, as if afraid a slice of bacon, like the Runaway Pancake, might decide to make a break for it. I wondered, as I stood watching from the doorway, what the past seven years would have been without her. Not nearly as interesting, I decided, or as full.

"You talk to Aunt Emma?" she asked.

"I did. She said I should talk to you."

She forgot the bacon for the moment. "About what?"

I poured myself a cup of coffee and took a seat at the table. "The McCorkle heirs."

"There aren't any that I know of."

"What about Simon McCorkle's oldest daughter? Esther, I believe her name is."

"What about her?" She began scooping bacon from the frying pan and laying the pieces on a paper towel.

"Aunt Emma said you two used to be thick once upon a time."

"We were," she agreed.

"What happened?"

"We fell out." She didn't want to talk about it.

"Over what?"

"Over a lot of things, none of which are any concern of yours." She opened the refrigerator and began shuffling jars around as if she were looking for something.

"They're on the counter," I said.

"What are?"

"The eggs."

"I know that. I'm looking for something else." But she didn't take anything from the refrigerator before closing the door.

"What all can you tell me about Esther McCorkle?" I persisted.

She glanced at me. I'd hit a sore spot in her life. "Why is it so important that I tell you about Esther McCorkle? What does she have to do with anything?"

"I'm trying to find out who owns that three acres along Lost Road where John Knight's house sits. I wondered if it's Esther McCorkle."

"It's not Esther McCorkle," she insisted.

"How can you be so certain?"

"Because Esther McCorkle's dead. She rowed herself out to the middle of Lake Mendota and jumped overboard several years ago."

"Suicide?"

67

She began breaking eggs into a bowl. "I don't know what else you'd call it. Esther could swim like a seal."

"Did she have any children?"

"One. That sickly girl of hers. But odds are against it that she ever lived past childhood."

"What about her husband?"

"She didn't have one." Ruth added salt, pepper, milk, and catsup, then began to beat the eggs. "She had the child out of wedlock by the owner of a huckster wagon that she ran away with. But before long he ran out on her and the baby, and she had to come back home with her tail between her legs."

"To Simon McCorkle?"

"Yes. To Simon McCorkle." Ruth's face showed little sympathy. "It liked to killed her, but she finally had to swallow some of that pride of hers."

"Was Simon McCorkle the s.o.b. Aunt Emma said he was?"

"That puts him too high on the ladder, if you're asking me."

"Why didn't you like him? Was it general principles or what?"

She turned down the fire under the skillet and added the eggs. "General principles, the way he treated his family, the way he looked, smelled, and acted—you name it. His children were no more than slaves to him, especially after his wife died. And once Esther made the mistake of coming back after running away, he made her life miserable. And if she even looked cross-eyed at him, he took his razor strap to her."

"What did Esther do in return?"

"Nothing. With a sickly child to raise, she had no other choice. But I knew Esther McCorkle well enough to know she didn't take it with a smile."

68

"Do you think she was the one who hung Simon on the hay hook?"

Taking a hot pad from the stove, she held onto the handle of the skillet while she worked the eggs.

"Ruth?" I said when I saw she wasn't going to answer.

"No comment."

"Meaning yes?"

"Meaning no comment."

"Whatever happened to Esther McCorkle?"

She abruptly turned to me. "I told you what happened to her. She drowned herself in the middle of Lake Mendota."

"Before that, I mean."

She turned her attention back to the eggs. "After Simon was murdered, the first thing she did was to sell all of Simon's land, which was quite a chunk in those days. Then she moved to Madison right about the time World War II was ending and went into the real estate business. From what I understand, she did well and ended up a rich woman."

"Did you ever see her again after she left here?"

"Once. At a class reunion, our thirty-fifth, I think. She was dressed to kill, wearing a fur of some kind, and enough jewelry to make her bowlegged." She put the eggs and bacon on a platter and turned out the fire under the skillet. "But underneath all that jewelry, makeup, and fur, and behind that one sleepy eye of hers, it was the same Esther, ramrod straight and hard as nails."

"Are you saying she hadn't mellowed over the years like you have?"

Setting the platter down in front of me, she said, "I'll pretend I didn't hear that."

I took off some scrambled eggs and bacon and

69

passed the platter on to Ruth. "Aunt Emma mentioned that Esther had a brother and a sister. Whatever happened to them?"

"Her brother Henry ran away from home at fifteen to join the navy. That's the last I heard of him."

"Then he's dead?"

"I don't know. I haven't kept track of him over the years."

"What about Esther's sister?"

Ruth set the platter down without taking anything from it. "No one knows what happened to her. She disappeared when she was twelve and hasn't been seen since."

"Just like that?" I snapped my fingers.

"Yes. Just like that."

"You're not eating," I observed.

"I'm not hungry," she answered.

"How old was Esther when her sister disappeared?" I asked.

"Fifteen, the same age I was. Why?"

"I just wondered." Taking a bite of scrambled eggs, I washed it down with a drink of coffee. "Will you do me a favor, Ruth? See if you can locate Henry McCorkle for me. That failing, you might try Esther McCorkle's daughter to see if she's still alive."

Her look said I'd better have a good reason for asking. "Even if I can find them, which I doubt, what good will that do? I thought you were looking for Diana, not digging up old bones from the past."

"I am looking for Diana," I said sharply. "But I have to start someplace."

"Why with Henry McCorkle, who to my knowledge hasn't set foot in Oakalla in the past fifty years? Or Esther McCorkle's daughter, who's probably long dead and buried?"

"Because I want to know who owns that property where John Knight was living. Maybe one of them can tell me."

"How will that help you find Diana?" she challenged me.

"Because whoever owns that property had to tell John Knight about it. He couldn't have found it on his own, not in a hundred years. It's too isolated."

"You told me he was a backwoodsman. Why couldn't he have found it on his own? It seems to me the most likely place for him to light."

"And build a house?" I asked.

"Why not?"

"Think about it, Ruth," I said, chewing on a piece of bacon. "How, out of all the available land in Adams County, did John Knight happen to build on the three acres that nobody seems to own?"

"I'm beginning to get your drift," she admitted.

"I hoped you would."

She took the platter of bacon and eggs and unloaded what was left of it onto her plate. "There is one other thing you might consider," she said. "That John Knight didn't land on that property by accident because he already owned it."

"I don't want to consider that possibility," I said. "Otherwise, then I might never find Diana."

"I'll see what I can do."

"Thanks, Ruth. I appreciate it."

Cool in the shade, warm in the sun, the morning promised another fine day. I spent all of it working on the *Oakalla Reporter* and writing my column, which I'd changed from an earlier idea to a discussion of the paranormal. As an entrenched man of reason, I hated to even bring up the subject because it evoked ghosts and goblins and things that went bump in the night. Never had I seen a ghost, goblin, gremlin, flying saucer, mutating cupcake, or carnivorous cheese ball for that matter. And though I knew a lot of people who had— sober, normal, everyday people who played bingo and paid taxes and went to church Christmas and Easter—I remained skeptical, preferring to believe that while they saw something, it wasn't what they thought they saw.

However, in my seven years with Ruth, and even before that with Grandmother Ryland, I'd developed a healthy respect for dreams, intuition, and though it was hard for me to admit it, feelings. At first when Ruth said she had a feeling about something, I'd smirk at the thought. No longer. Though her feelings weren't always right on target, coupled with her dreams, they usually approached the truth closely enough for me to wonder. And when she said she had a burden for somebody, as with Grandmother Ryland in the past, more times than not that person was already in, or headed for, trouble. So I decided to share my thoughts and my doubts with my readers to see what they had to say about the paranormal.

Interrupted by a dozen phone calls, I finished the first draft of my column about noon, then went uptown to the Corner Bar and Grill for lunch. After ordering baked steak, mashed potatoes and gravy, pea salad, and milk, I helped myself to one of Sniffy Smith's onion rings, while he picked up the nearest ashtray and carried it to the far end of the counter. A former smoker himself during most of the years he barbered, Sniffy suddenly couldn't stand the smell of cigarette smoke and began sniffing loudly whenever he encountered it.

Sniffy returned to his seat at the counter, munching down a stray potato chip he'd found along the way. Then I noticed him studying me. "It's my beard," I said.

"That's what's different about me." I couldn't remember the last time I'd shaved.

He shook his head. "Nope. That ain't it. I saw you with a beard before during the centennial celebration. This is different. It's in your eyes. You look older somehow."

"Maybe I'm just tired."

"And maybe it's more than that," he said. "I saw a lot of men who came back from the Second World War. They had that same look in their eyes."

"What look is that?"

"'Discomboodled' is the word I made up for it, since nothing else seemed to fit. It's like somebody just turned the clock up while you weren't looking. None of your old clothes fit anymore."

I didn't like talking about it. "You're right, Sniffy. That's about where I am."

He picked up his breaded tenderloin. "Any particular reason why?"

"Diana's missing, and no one seems to know where she is."

He sat up and sniffed loudly. "Diana Baldwin?"

We then had everyone's attention. "Yes."

"For how long has she been missing?"

"Over a week." Closer to two, if I were honest with myself.

"Any idea where she is?"

Bernice brought my order and set it on the table in front of me. "No. No idea at all."

"Then why ain't you out looking for her?" he persisted.

"Because," I said slowly, choking on the frustration, "I don't know where the hell to look."

"What about Sheriff Roberts; he have any ideas where to look?"

I took a bite of baked steak and shoved it aside. "Let's just forget it, Sniffy. I don't want to talk about it."

He hunched over the counter, ignoring his lunch. I got the message. His feelings were hurt, and he wasn't going to speak until spoken to.

"Find Henry McCorkle for me," I said. "If you really want to help."

He brightened. "That's easy enough. He's in the navy. At least he was the last time I saw him."

"When was that?"

He began counting to himself. "Fifteen, twenty years ago, I'd say. He stuck his head in the shop to say hey, did I know who he was. Of course I knew who he was. There's only one Henry McCorkle."

"Thanks, Sniffy," I said, rising from my seat.

"Where are you going? You're not even half-done with your lunch."

"To make a phone call. You're welcome to help yourself if you like."

He eyed the baked steak hungrily. "Only until you get back."

I called Ruth at home and told her what Sniffy had told me. She said she'd look into it. On my way out of the Corner Bar and Grill, I noticed Sniffy had made short work of my baked steak and mashed potatoes and gravy. I waved good-bye. He smiled sheepishly and shrugged.

Later that night I had the *Oakalla Reporter* ready to print and the beginning of a headache. The act of working on the *Oakalla Reporter*, blocking it, laying it out, filling, cutting, editing, trying to get the columns and pages to balance was always a challenge no matter how often I'd done it. But when it all finally fell together, when I could look at it from the outside and

74

see what I'd done, I felt immense satisfaction, like snapping in the last piece of a jigsaw puzzle.

Rupert came into my office and stood by the window that looked out on Gas Line Road. A breeze blew in, rustling the papers on my desk. Warm and mellow, it smelled like the first day of school.

"It's a long, long way from May to December," I said.

He didn't answer for a while. Like mine, his thoughts were elsewhere. "Clarkie's had no luck locating John Knight or anybody that fits his description," he said. "With all the time that's passed, you'd think we would have run across something by now."

Together we watched the moon rise in the east. Thin and yellow, it wore a fuzzy skirt of clouds. "You think he might have done that before?" I asked. "Raped and run?"

"We don't know for a fact that he did," Rupert said. "But if it's true that Devin LeMay ran across him somewhere up north in the wilderness, chances are he was up there for a reason."

"Like laying low?"

"I wouldn't bet against it."

"Neither would I, from what I've learned about him."

Finished with the moon, Rupert turned his attention to me. "How are you holding up?"

"Fine, I guess," I said. "Today I've been too busy to think about it."

"Maybe you should go somewhere this weekend," he suggested. "Get away and rest your mind for a while."

"Maybe I should," I answered. "But I doubt I will."

He nodded in understanding. "I'll let you know if we come up with anything."

"There is one place you might try," I said. "See if anyone in the military is looking for John Knight."

"Funny, I was just about to do that tomorrow."

"You know what they say about great minds."

He took out his tobacco pouch and put a chew into his mouth. "Then we're both in trouble."

As Rupert left, my printer came in. Except to nod and say hello, we rarely spoke to each other until the *Oakalla Reporter* was out. He had his job to do, and he preferred I let him do it. While waiting for him to set the type and start the press in motion, I remembered with a smile waiting for my very first *Oakalla Reporter* to come off the press. It was like waiting for my son to be born—tick-tock, tick-tock, look at the clock and pace the room, tick-tock, tick-tock, look at the clock and pace some more.

When each finally arrived, my joy was complete. My son died on his first birthday, and my life stopped until I moved to Oakalla to start it over again. But my seven years with the *Oakalla Reporter*, watching it take its first few awkward steps, then take off in its own direction with its own identity, had been a wonder and a delight. My brainchild. My only child, as it turned out.

*Freedom's Voice*, the forerunner of the *Oakalla Reporter*, was preceded by the *Oakalla Banner*, in many ways the true ancestor of the *Oakalla Reporter*.

When I had occasion to read the old issues, I usually discovered something new about the past and something more about myself, which I couldn't say about most of the things I read.

Scanning its brittle pages, I learned that McCorkle Chapel had burned, and Hattie McCorkle, Esther and Henry McCorkle's younger sister, had disappeared during the last week of July in 1933. Lightning had struck McCorkle Chapel and set it afire; Hattie McCorkle's disappearance was blamed on the same thunderstorm that had destroyed the chapel. "A simpleminded girl terrified of storms," Hattie was home alone when the storm hit. Consensus was that the storm unnerved her to the point that she "fled from home in terror," and didn't return. I wondered why even a simpleminded girl would run from her home out into a storm, and why, even though she was never found, the *Oakalla Banner* didn't mention Hattie McCorkle again.

The first paper came off the press. I picked it up and smelled it. Still warm, it had a smell like no other. I took it into my office to look it over. A few minutes later my printer joined me there, taking his usual seat atop my desk with a cup of thermos coffee beside him, while he read my column. "Well?" I asked when he finished.

"That should stir things up" was all he said.

"You done for the night?"

"I'm done," he said, rolling up the paper. "Except for putting the labels on and taking the papers to the post office."

"I'll give you a hand."

"No," he insisted. "You go home and get some sleep. You look like you could use it."

"I can," I admitted. "Al," I said before he left. "Do you put much stock in feelings?"

"Some. About the same as you do, I reckon."

"Then I have the feeling you might be going it alone next Thursday night."

"Why? You planning a trip somewhere?"

"Somewhere. But I don't know where yet."

"Business or pleasure trip?" he asked.

"Business. I'm going to try to find Diana Baldwin."

"Sniffy said she was missing." He shrugged. "I'll do my best to see that the paper gets out."

# 6

Henry McCorkle lived in a veterans' home on a bluff high above the Wisconsin River. Below, the river wound through canyons and around sandbars, meandering along like it had all eternity to get where it was going; ahead, the drive up to the veterans' home climbed and curved around a postcard-perfect lawn of spruce and hemlock. The home itself had been built on three levels as it followed the contour of the bluff. Rising in natural progression with the rock beneath it, the walls of the home seemed a harmonious and integral part of the bluff, rather than an appendage man had tacked on. Recalling John Knight's house along Lost Road, how it violated the natural harmony of both man and nature, I saw the difference in vision between a clear mind and a troubled one.

I parked Jessie in the shade of a blue spruce and went to find the office. The receptionist directed me to the person in charge of visitors, and she directed me to the recreation room, where a group of nurses sat at a table drinking coffee and eating potato chips. Except for them, the recreation room was empty.

Approaching the table of nurses, I felt like I was back in college again, trying to put the move on somebody. And when all of them looked up at me at once, I felt my face redden. Going solo into a lions' den seemed a lot easier.

"You lost?" one of them asked. Their ages varied from twenty to fifty, but on all their faces I saw that becalmed I've-seen-it-all look that nurses wear.

"Probably," I answered.

They waited for me to go on. I waited for one of them to give me an opening. Finally one of them did. "Let me guess. You heard about the food here. But as you can see, this table is taken."

"Actually I came to see Henry McCorkle. Do any of you happen to know where he is?"

Looking at one another in turn, each shrugged. "What do you want with Henry?" the youngest one asked.

"I just want to talk to him. I run a newspaper in Oakalla, which is Henry's hometown, and I'm looking for a missing person, actually several missing persons, but one in particular. I think Henry can help me find her."

"Is this missing person a friend of yours?"

"You might say that, yes."

"Is Henry a friend of yours?"

"I didn't know Henry McCorkle existed until two days ago."

"Then what can Henry possibly have to do with your missing friend?"

I told them as best I could. When I finished, the

oldest of them said, "You'll find Henry in his room. Tell Mrs. Lundquist I said it was okay."

"Thanks. I appreciate it."

"Don't get your hopes up," she cautioned.

"Why? Is there something about Henry I should know?"

The youngest one looked at the others. "Henry is . . . Well, he's Henry. That's the best I can put it. You'll soon see for yourself."

I soon saw for myself. Wearing only his jockey shorts, Henry McCorkle sat on the edge of his bed playing solitaire, cursing each turn of the cards whether it helped him or not. Then he had a dry run where nothing turned up, as his curses grew louder and stronger and the veins on his neck popped out. Finally, to get to the jack of clubs, he played the three of diamonds on the four of hearts. "There, by God!" he said. "How do you like them apples!" Even though the play didn't help him in the end, he seemed infinitely satisfied for having made it.

"You could have uncovered the jack of clubs by playing the three of diamonds on the four of spades," I pointed out.

Henry McCorkle noticed me for the first time. He had a pointed nose, narrow shoulders, a sunken chest that was as bare as his arms, and the whitest skin I'd ever seen on anyone. Thin and birdlike, he couldn't have weighed much over a hundred pounds even though he appeared at least six feet tall. "Hell, I know that, sonny," he said. "But that would be taking the easy way out."

"You'd rather cheat, is that it?"

He smiled at me, revealing a gap where his two lower front teeth should have been. "If I have to. In cards, like in life, you do whatever's necessary."

81

"To win?" I asked.

"Sometimes," he answered with a twinkle in his eyes. "But not always. Sometimes it's just to make things interesting until something better comes along. Which, if a man's patient enough, it usually does."

"May I quote you on that?"

"Hell, you can do with that whatever you want, sonny. Pearls of wisdom. Henry McCorkle's full of them. Just make sure you spell my name right," he added. "It's McCorkle, two c's with a cap on the second one. Just like what's on my uniform," he said, patting his bare chest.

"Your nametag's a little hard to read," I said. "You got any with bigger letters?"

"You see?" he yelled to someone passing in the hall. "I ain't as crazy as you think. It's just that none of you chickenshit bastards have a sense of humor, that's all." He got up and slammed the door to his room. Then he smiled impishly at me. "Let them think I'm throwing a fit. That'll keep the kettle simmering until I think of something else."

"Why?" I asked him.

"Why not?" he answered brightly. "What's your name, sonny?"

"Garth Ryland."

"Pleased to meet you. I'm Henry McCorkle." We shook hands. His was long and bony, scarred in several places. "It's like this, Garth Ryland," he went on. "What if I was to be like everyone else that's in this place, shell-shocked, or paralyzed, or dying of cancer. Alone, I might add. Most of us veterans are. What would be the point in that? I was never cold sober a day in my life. By that I mean square to the world's way of thinking. What's the use in starting now?"

I nodded, thinking he was finished.

"Hell, I got busted from chief to seaman more times than any man I know, probably more times than any man in the history of the U.S. Navy. But they kept kicking me back up to chief again. Do you know why?" His chest swelled as much as it could. "Because the chiefs run the navy, and Henry McCorkle was one of the best damn chiefs the navy ever had. It's just those chickenshit rules he couldn't abide by. They were made for somebody else, not Henry McCorkle."

Not Garth Ryland either, if the truth were known. "So why did you stay in?"

"That's easy enough to answer. I was fifteen when I went in, sixty-two when I came out. Where else with no education and no trade to speak of could I get three squares, free room and board for forty-seven years, and get paid a little something besides. The question you should be asking is why I ever bothered to get out."

"Okay, why did you get out?"

He glanced around the room, white and bare, except for his bed, footlocker, and a small writing desk and chair. No books, television, or radio that I could see. "Hell, I don't know why I got out. I should have waited for them to drum me out proper. I'm bored stiff here and afraid that if I went out into the real world, one of those eighteen-wheelers would run over me and squash me flat as a bug there on the Interstate. So here I sit day after day, for going on nine years now, trying to keep things stirred up and not go crazy at the same time."

"You should move back to Oakalla," I suggested. "I think you'd find a home there."

"Among all those landlubbers?" he snorted. "What would we have in common?"

"You might be surprised," I said.

"I'll think on it. But probably not too hard." Then

his eyes narrowed and hardened, tiny specks of red showing. "How did you know I'm from Oakalla? Only a handful of people know that, and you ain't one of them."

"Ruth Krammes, my housekeeper, told me. She and your sister Esther used to be good friends."

Delighted, he slapped his hand on his knee. "Hell, yes, I remember Ruth, even though she was only a kid when I left home. A real spitfire she was. Tall and slim with that something in her eyes that said not to cross her path unless you were prepared to have some heavy damage done to you. And contrary," he said shaking his head. "I never met such a contrary person before or since. And not shy either about speaking her mind." He shook his head again. "Good lord, yes, I remember her!"

I had to smile. "Don't tell her I said this, but she hasn't changed much over the years."

"Nobody ever does," he said philosophically. "Only our appearance, that's all. Take my sister Esther. From the time I first remember her to the last time I saw her, she never opened one window in that cold heart of hers."

Seizing the opportunity, I asked, "When was the last time you saw Esther?"

He sat on the edge of his bed with his long legs tucked under him. "Probably eight, nine years ago, not long after I came here. I knew from the minute I saw her what she was after, but I'd already made up my mind she wasn't going to get it."

"What was she after?" I asked.

"The deed!" he shouted as if I should know. "For service rendered during the Civil War, Abraham Lincoln granted my grandfather Silas McCorkle three hundred and twenty acres of prime land there in Adams

84

County. Has Abraham Lincoln's own signature right there on the deed. It's not one of those forged jobs where one of his lackeys signed it, like they do today. I took it to a man who knew."

"How did you come by it?" I asked, because Henry McCorkle had run away from home at fifteen.

"I stole it," he said without apology or regret. "Took it off the wall the night I left home. I knew that if there was one thing that would get my father's goat, drive that old sonofabitch crazy, it would be for me to take that deed. That was the only thing he managed to rescue the night my grandfather Silas's house burned down, killing Silas and four of his five children." He paused, so I wouldn't miss his point. "That deed and Silas's wife, who he later married." His eyes simmered as he spoke. "There's one thing you need to know about the McCorkles, sonny. They're the most possessive bastards on earth. And they ain't above killing you or anybody else to keep what they think is rightfully theirs." Then he smiled, rocking back on his heels like a benevolent sage. "There's another thing you should know about the McCorkles, too. They don't show their age like other people do. Leastwise, all of us except Esther, who was looking pretty shopworn the last time I saw her. Hell, I'm seventy-one-years-old," he continued. "I'll bet I don't look a day over fifty, do I?"

"Closer to forty-five," I agreed, though he looked about sixty to me.

He slapped his thigh in delight. "You see. What did I tell you! Seventy-one-years-old and I've still got all of my hair and most of my teeth." He winked at me. "And all the lead in my pencil, too, if you want to know the truth of the matter."

I smiled, hoping that at seventy-one I still had

Henry McCorkle's verve. "Does the deed you stole have any value other than to a McCorkle?" I asked.

"It's got Abraham Lincoln's signature on it. That must be worth something," he said. "But no, the deed itself is worthless. There ain't nothing left of that property but the three acres where the old McCorkle home place used to sit. At least that's what Esther told me. She had no reason to lie."

"Where the cemetery is?" I asked, wanting to be sure.

"Right. Where the cemetery is. That's all that place was good for anyway, burying people."

"Do you know who owns that three acres now?" I asked.

"I do." He reddened, showing his embarrassment. "Or at least I did, until that wolf in sheep's clothing stole it from me."

"Your sister Esther?"

He shook his head. "No. Though she'd qualify if anybody would. It was that college boy they had working here, the one who was all laughs and smiles until your back was turned. Then his true colors came out." Taking himself to task, Henry McCorkle didn't spare any feelings. "I knew from the minute I first saw him. I said to myself, Henry McCorkle, there's somebody who bears watching because there's fangs showing just beneath that smile of his." He smacked his fist into his hand in anger. "I had him pegged dead right, too, and still he made off with my deed. After that none of us here ever saw him again."

"Do you remember what he looked like?" I asked.

"Like a wolf in sheep's clothing," he answered. "Just like I said he did."

"Nothing in particular that stood out about him?" I was thinking of John Knight's beard.

"His fangs," he said. "Ready to take the hide right off of you." Then he smiled at me. "I know what you're asking, sonny. But for the life of me I can't picture that little sonofabitch. Like a McCorkle, I'm tempted to say, but I know I'm the only one of us left."

"Did this happen before or after your sister Esther came to visit?" I asked.

He thought a moment, then said, "It had to be after. Because I still had the deed at the time, and she wanted it. She said she didn't want it for herself but someone else, that it was his birthright and we owed it to him."

"*His* birthright? I thought she had a daughter."

"So did I. And if I have my facts straight, she died at an early age. But I'd swear on a stack of Bibles she said *his* birthright. It took me by surprise, too."

"Do you have any idea whom she might have meant?"

He shook his head. "None whatsoever. Like I said, as far as I know I'm the last of the McCorkles."

"What about your sister Hattie?"

Pursing his lips, he glanced up at the ceiling. "Lord knows what happened to Hattie, her being so timid and feebleminded and all. What people don't know about her is that she was once the brightest and the best of the lot. Then one day while cutting a switch for one of the horses that was balking on him, my father cut through the reins and away they went, throwing him overboard. My mother, Esther, and Hattie were in the back of the wagon, and my mother knew the horses would make the turn for home, likely turning the wagon over on them, so she jumped out with instructions for Esther to hand Hattie to her while she galloped along beside the wagon. Of course Mother fell flat on her face when she landed. Esther panicked and jumped out of the wagon right after Mother did, landing on Hattie, who she was holding in her arms. After that Hattie was never the same." He wore a bittersweet smile. "Do you know what the funny part is?" he said. "The horses never made the turn for home at all. They just ran into an oat field and stopped there."

Several seconds went by before I asked, "Did you or any of your family ever hear from Hattie again after she disappeared?"

"Not to my knowledge. I'd already joined the navy when it happened. Whatever information I did get about her was always secondhand. I didn't even know she was missing until Sniffy Smith wrote to tell me about a year later." Suddenly he met me squarely with a hard stare, revealing a side of Henry McCorkle I hadn't seen before. Like the rest of the McCorkles, he could play hardball when he wanted to. "Since I've been so free with you, why don't you answer me this question. Why the sudden interest in the McCorkles?"

I told him why I was interested in the McCorkles. When I finished, he said, "I sure wish I could help you, sonny, but that missing girl of yours . . . Well, I wouldn't know where to tell you to look."

I rose, preparing to leave. "Thanks, Henry," I said. "You've been a big help regardless."

"Sorry I couldn't have been more of one." Picking up his deck of cards, he began to play solitaire again, cursing every turn of the cards as before. Then he winked at me. "You can leave the door open when you go. You bastard!" was the last thing I heard as I left.

Jenny Carter wasn't expecting company. Wearing a white bikini and carrying a beach towel, she gasped when she opened the door and saw me standing there. Evidently she hadn't forgotten me in the three days that had passed since my last visit.

"What are you doing back here?" she demanded.

"I was on my way home from somewhere and decided to stop by. I hope I haven't come at a bad time."

"I was just about to go swimming," she said. "But I guess it can wait."

"You're sure? I can always come back later."

"No. Now is fine," she insisted. She eyed me warily. "Unless you've come with bad news about Devin."

"I don't know any more about Devin's whereabouts than I did before," I said. "I'm here because I want to borrow the key to his house again."

"Why?"

"To have another look around."

"Where?"

"The basement in particular. We never got that far if I remember right."

"Why do you want to look in Devin's basement?"

I told her why.

She shrugged, as if it were of no concern to her. "I'll go get the key."

I waited outside while she went after it. Again I heard something thumping in the wind. It sounded a little closer than before.

"Do you have something in your attic?" I asked Jenny on her return.

"We have a lot of things in our attic," she replied curtly. "Is there anything in particular you had in mind?"

"It sounds like something's trapped up there. Maybe a squirrel or a bat."

"I think it's a bat," she answered, seeming to like the idea the more she thought about it. "Anyway, something's been keeping me up nights."

"Do you mind if I take a look?"

She slowly shook her head. "No. Not if you'll lead the way. I hate bats. I have ever since one bit me when I was a little girl."

She followed me up a curving flight of stairs to a landing, then up a shorter, narrower flight of stairs to the attic. I stopped at the top of the stairs. She stopped right behind me, where I could smell her musky scent, feel the warmth ebb from her sleek supple body. With no one else around, it was hard not to imagine the possibilities.

I went on into the attic. Jenny followed, turning on a dim bulb that did little to help me see beyond the next shadow. If Diana was in there, I couldn't find her. Neither did I find the bat Jenny had told me about. The attic baked in the afternoon sun. I began to sweat. So did Jenny Carter. She glistened in the dim light, made purring sounds as she rubbed against me. Less than a yard away a mattress leaned against a rafter. I glanced from it to Jenny Carter, who looked right at me, not trying to hide her need. I wanted her, because I had my own need that hadn't been met for a long time. We didn't have to love or even like each other to give the other what each wanted. And I doubted either one of us would walk away feeling guilty.

"We'd better go downstairs," I said.

She didn't give up easily. "Why? Who would we hurt?"

I didn't have a good answer for her. "You mean who haven't already hurt us?"

"Yes. I guess that's what I mean."

"I'm not sure I know." I made myself take a step toward the staircase. "But then you never know."

"No," she said huskily. "You don't."

Once outside I said, "I'd better go into Devin's alone."

She handed me the key. "Whatever you like," she said dully. "I'll be on the pier."

"Where should I leave the key?"

"With me. I'll see that it gets back where it belongs."

Entering Devin LeMay's house for the second time, I saw that nothing had changed from before. Gnats peppered the wineglasses, rose in a puff from the blackened bananas. Flies buzzed against the screens, either wanting in or out. Wolf spiders patrolled the counters and basins, while other spiders hung their webs in the corners and passageways. An air of must and longing still lingered in spite of the open windows. A wave of disconsolation still rode upon my shoulders. The walls were still white, the wainscoting black, the door to Mother LeMay's room still locked.

Raising the small metal door serving her room, I asked, "Mother LeMay, are you in there?" When no one answered, I closed the door with a bang and went on my way.

Devin LeMay's basement had been paneled with white birch and furnished with a couch, carpet, easy chair, and color television. It also contained a small workshop, along with an ample supply of hand and power tools that seemed in perfect repair. Beyond the workshop a bedroom had been set off by itself, and furnished with a soft blue carpet and curtains to match the furniture. Women's clothes filled the closet and chest of drawers, and judging by their labels, had cost more than anything else in the basement. Apparently Mother LeMay led a double life. Either that or Devin and Helen Carter LeMay had separate bedrooms.

"Satisfied?" Jenny Carter asked when I returned Devin LeMay's key to her. She sat on his pier in a yard chair facing the sun. In her sunglasses and white bikini, she'd already attracted the attention of a couple of water-skiers who were shooting close to the pier, doing their best to impress her.

"It seems you have an audience," I said.

"I wish they'd get the hell out of here," she snapped. "If Devin were around, you can bet he wouldn't stand for it."

"What would Devin do?" I asked. "Shake his fist at them?" Despite the set of weights in his bedroom, Devin LeMay didn't seem very physical to me. But then I'd never seen him with his clothes off as Diana had.

"Drive his boat right over their ski rope like he has before," she said. "They know they're not supposed to be in this close to shore." The thought of Devin LeMay driving away her suitors made her smile.

"I don't see Devin's boat," I observed.

She glanced sharply at the empty boathouse. "I forgot. Devin's been having trouble with his motor. It's at the marina."

"I thought he might have taken it up north with him."

She turned to glare at one of the skiers who passed within a ski length of the pier. "He might have at that. But I know it's been gone most of the summer."

"It's hard to be a white knight without a charger."

"What's that?" She glared at the water-skier, who had the nerve to wave back at her.

"Nothing. Sorry to bother you."

She looked up at me. But I couldn't see her eyes through her sunglasses. "I'll bet," she said.

"Meaning?"

She shifted her gaze to an incoming boat and skier. "The way Diana told it to Devin, you're supposed to be some kind of superman detective. All I can say is, you couldn't prove it by me."

As the boat roared by, the skier sent a plume of water our way. Most of it landed on Jenny. "God damn you!" she yelled at him. She took off her sunglasses to wipe her face. I noticed she'd been crying.

"Is something the matter?" I asked.

"No!" she snapped. "Nothing's the matter!" She rose from her chair and took her towel with her. "As you can see, with those idiots out there, everything's just fine and dandy."

"I mean besides them."

She put her sunglasses back on, again hiding her eyes from me. "Isn't it obvious?" she asked. "I want Devin home, and I want him home *now*."

"I'll see what I can do," I promised without conviction.

But I doubted she heard me. Jenny Carter burst into tears and ran for the house.

On the way home hopelessness overtook me, and I sank lower than I had for years, lower even than the day my divorce was finally final and I left Milwaukee to come to Oakalla to try to start my life over. Then I remembered the day my son died, and the ice cream truck that was playing the "Camptown Races" as it went by outside, and I sank lower still. But thanks to Sheriff Rupert Roberts, who sat at my kitchen table with a chew in his mouth and a smile in his eyes, my feeling of hopelessness ended there.

# 7

*I* rose at dawn the next morning and packed an all-weather suitcase that included my wool shirt, bib overalls, compass, and rain suit. Rupert hadn't found John Knight, but he thought he'd located John Knight's parents, Seth and Clover Richwine, who lived on a small farm near Gunther, Iowa, about a hundred miles southwest of Oakalla. Jack Richwine was John Knight's real name. He'd gone A.W.O.L. from the army ten years before to escape rape charges pending against him, and hadn't been captured. Six feet tall with black hair, blue-black eyes, and a beard to match, Jack Richwine had, among other things, been described by the military police as extremely dangerous, and by his commanding officer as a wolf in sheep's clothing.

Ruth had risen before I did and had a platter of sausage and pancakes sitting on the table when I came down the stairs. Taking a bottle of real Wisconsin maple syrup from the cupboard, she set it in front of me along with a cup of coffee and a glass of orange juice.

"I should leave every day," I said.

"Just make sure you come back," she answered.

I noted her worried look. "Why wouldn't I come back?" I asked.

"Just be careful," she said, avoiding the question.

"As if what I say matters."

I put some pancakes and sausage on my plate and covered them with syrup. "Ruth, I have a favor," I said. "I don't know where I'll end up or when I'll get back, because I'm not stopping with Gunther, Iowa, no matter what happens there. So if I don't get back in time, I want you to see what you can do about putting the *Oakalla Reporter* out. I've already talked to Al Hanneman, my printer, and he'll help in any way he can."

"Don't talk with your mouth full," she said.

"Will you do it?"

She got up to pour herself a second cup of coffee. "We'll see when the time comes," she said. "You might be back before you know it."

"Or it could be weeks."

She shrugged but didn't answer. Neither one of us really wanted to talk about it.

"Did you find out anything more about Esther McCorkle's daughter?" I asked.

"Yes," she answered. "She's dead. She died when she was ten, according to the Dane County records."

"You're sure about that?"

"Dane County is sure about that. Why?" she asked.

"Henry McCorkle said that Esther paid him a visit eight or nine years ago, wanting the original land grant deed that Abraham Lincoln had signed over to Silas McCorkle, Henry's grandfather. Esther wanted it for a boy, according to Henry. She said it was his birthright."

95

"Meaning what?" Ruth asked.

"Meaning where did the boy come from if Esther's only child died when she was ten years old?"

Ruth thought about it momentarily, then dismissed it. "I wouldn't put too much stock in what Henry McCorkle says. In the old days he was lucky to tell a frog from a chipmunk."

"He had you pegged about right," I said.

She reddened. "What did Henry McCorkle say about me?"

"Nothing that you haven't heard before from me. I was more interested in what he had to say about Hattie McCorkle."

Her blush began to pale. "Which was?"

"That she was the brightest and the best of the McCorkles until Esther jumped out of a runaway wagon and landed on her."

Ruth got busy at the stove. "I wouldn't know," she said.

"And I think I know why the name McCorkle jumped out at me," I continued. "Isn't Hattie McCorkle the one who's supposed to haunt Lost Road?"

Ruth warmed my coffee for something to do. "It's possible," she agreed. But she didn't offer an explanation.

"How did all that get started anyway?"

"How did all what get started?" She didn't want to discuss it.

"The part about Hattie haunting Lost Road. Was she seen along there?"

Returning to the table, Ruth cut into her pancakes, but then left her fork on her plate. "She was said to have been seen along there several times," Ruth answered. "But never by me."

"Or Esther either?"

96

"What does Esther have to do with it?" she said with a flare of anger.

"A theory I have. Henry told me the McCorkles were the most possessive people on earth. So, say Esther had her designs on the McCorkle estate, three hundred and twenty acres worth, which was quite a lot in those days. If Simon died, what would stand in the way between her and it?"

"Henry McCorkle for one," Ruth pointed out.

"But Henry was in the navy and not likely to return to claim his share even if he wanted it, which he obviously didn't." I smiled at Ruth. She didn't smile back. "Whom does that leave?"

"You know who it leaves," she answered. "The fly in your ointment is that Hattie McCorkle didn't have sense enough to want the land, or to know how to go about getting it, even if she did."

"But Hattie probably knew enough to attract a husband someday," I said. "There are a lot of men, now and then, who would have married her for the land."

"Agreed," Ruth said, warming to the task. "But why, then, did Esther run off with a huckster when she finally had things going all her way?"

"That's the part I can't figure out," I said.

She took a bite of her pancakes. "When you do, let me know."

"But that didn't stop Esther from coming back to Simon McCorkle later," I continued. "After she and the huckster didn't work out."

Ruth sat back in her chair with a disgusted look. "So then Esther bided her time, killed Simon with a two-by-four, and hung him on a hay hook to dry."

"Nobody said anything about a two-by-four," I pointed out.

Avoiding me, she leaned forward to cut another wedge out of her stack of pancakes. "I know."

After promising Jessie a bath, oil change, tune-up, and four new tires if she'd take me wherever we ended up going and back again in one piece, I left for Gunther, Iowa. Crossing the Mississippi River at Prairie du Chien, I continued on west through hills and dales, fields and woodlots, an occasional farm and an occasional town, much like the Wisconsin I'd left behind. An early spring followed by a dry summer made the fields look harvest-ready, more like mid-October than early September. Stunted and blanched rows of corn bled into fields of brown beans. Dark clover cured in windrows, and dusky moss clogged the ponds. Even the trees drooped low to the ground, as though they, too, were tired of summer, ready for fall.

Gunther, Iowa, had a population of three thousand and six, wide streets, wide-pillared porches on nearly all of its white houses, three stoplights, a drive-in restaurant at the east edge of town, a corner drugstore and a movie theater downtown, a silver water tower that I could see from ten miles out, and an air of hard-earned contentment. Gunther's town marshal was painting a fire hydrant silver and red in front of the town hall. I stopped to ask him directions to Seth and Clover Richwine's farm.

"What is it you wanted to see the Richwines about?" he asked, noting my Wisconsin license plate. Wearing a badge, but no gun, beads of sweat on his ruddy face, and a sweat-stained blue uniform that probably fit him two years ago, he worked with an ease that belied his weight. His eyes, young, friendly, and direct, said he knew what he was about and not to overlook that fact. I'd met men like him before. If you didn't push him, he wouldn't push back. If you did push him, you would wish you hadn't.

"You missed a spot," I said.

"Where's that?"

"On the cap. I'm looking at it now."

He dipped his brush into the can of silver paint and quickly painted over the spot. "Much obliged," he said. "But you still haven't told me why you want to see the Richwines."

"I'm looking for Jack Richwine."

He wasn't surprised. "So's the army. They send a man around here every year to see if Jack's come home." He set the brush and paint down and stood up. Standing, he was an even bigger man, and much less fat, than he had first appeared. "So why bother the Richwines with something they don't know anything about?"

"Meaning that if the army can't find him, then neither can I?" I asked.

He wiped the sweat from his forehead. "That about sums it up."

"What if I were to tell you I know where Jack Richwine was for certain three years ago, and I have a half-baked idea of where he is now."

"That won't cut any ice," he said. "Unless you tell me why you're looking for him."

I told him why. "If you want references, call Sheriff Rupert Roberts in Oakalla, Wisconsin. My name is Garth Ryland."

"I know," he said. "Sheriff Roberts called me early this morning to tell me you'd probably be by."

I smiled. Leave it to Rupert to look out for me. "Did Sheriff Roberts give me a good recommendation?"

"Good enough," he answered, reaching for his

99

paint can. Then he told me where I could find Seth and Clover Richwine.

"One question," I said. "What's your opinion of Jack Richwine?"

He knelt and started painting again. "I went through twelve years of school with Jack Richwine. I try not to have an opinion."

"Do you think he's capable of rape and murder?"

"I'd say the army has a good case against him."

"He's only wanted for rape by the army."

Feathering out the paint, he carefully avoided leaving any brush marks. "I know that. By not answering your question, I think I answered it."

"Is that a yes or a no? Is Jack Richwine capable of murder or not?"

He looked up at me and smiled, but I could still see the blue steel beneath it. "Take your pick," he said.

The farm of Seth and Clover Richwine looked worse than any of the surrounding farms, as though it had suffered through a twenty-year drought. Rocks showed in the pasture, which was eaten down to bare earth; ravelings of white paint hung from the house, and the once-white silo had a gray beard down to its knees. Pigeons came and went at will through the barn's broken windows, as a small herd of holsteins, like bedouins around an oasis, gathered around a salt block and took turns licking it.

I knocked on the back screen door of the house. When no one answered, I knocked again. The second time I heard approaching footsteps, though they stopped just short of the door. "Who is it?" a woman asked.

"Garth Ryland. I'm looking for Jack."

She opened the door and stepped outside. Tall and thin, she blinked constantly, her weak blue eyes watering in the sunlight. "Jack isn't here," she said. And could have added, "So why don't you leave us alone."

I studied her. Something wasn't quite right about her. For one thing she looked too pale to be a farmwife. For another her curly brown hair was too young for her face. Then I realized she wore a wig.

"I know he isn't," I said. "I was hoping you might know where he was."

"You a cop?" Her voice had no inflection, as though the life had been squeezed out of it.

"No."

"The army, then?"

"No. My name is Garth Ryland. I run a small newspaper in Oakalla, Wisconsin."

"Wisconsin, you say?"

I could have said New Zealand. Both seemed equally distant to her. "Yes. Oakalla's about a hundred miles northeast of here."

"Then what brings you all this way looking for Jack?"

I told her the truth.

She thought a moment, then said, "Why don't you come inside. The sun hurts my eyes."

I followed her inside through the back porch into the kitchen. Hot and close, the kitchen had yellow walls, one small window, and a linoleum floor. Not unlike Grandmother Ryland's kitchen, and a lot of other farm kitchens I knew, it was not at its best in summer. But come winter, with bread in the oven, the snow deep and rippled, and the wind at the windows, it would be downright cozy in there.

Seth Richwine sat in the living room under a dim light reading a Western. Gaunt and unshaven with short gray hair and extra-large ears that looked as though they'd been glued on, he took no notice of me.

"Seth, we have company," Clover Richwine said.

He glanced up at me, his eyes bright and fierce, like those of a falcon. "So we do," he said. Then he coughed violently, bending over and clutching his chest. I recognized the cough. My Uncle Charlie had one just like it. My Uncle Charlie died from emphysema.

"Have a seat," he said, laying the Western down.

I sat on the couch facing him. Clover Richwine sat on the other end of the couch, as far away from Seth Richwine as possible. Solidly built, deep burgundy in color, the couch had lost most of its nap, like a dog with mange.

"Sorry to bother you," I said to break the silence. Neither responded. Both sat there heavily, expectantly, like Frost's two tramps in mud time. "How are the crops this year?" I heard myself asking.

"No crops, just cows," Seth answered. "We cash-rent this place. Do our own milking, though."

"How are the cows, then?"

"Not good. Had a bout with mastitis this spring. Lost my best milker and her calf. Then the drought nearly burned up our pasture. Can't afford hay at the price it is, so either we've got to slaughter or sell before winter."

I thought of the holsteins I'd seen gathered around the salt block. It seemed they deserved a better fate. "No other choice?" I asked.

Seth Richwine leaned back in his chair, picked up an unlit pipe, and began to suck on it. "We could always let them starve to death."

Again they waited for me to speak. They looked like they'd been waiting all their lives—for the good life that never came. "I'm sorry," I said.

"So am I," Seth Richwine answered. "Sometimes that's all that's left to be." Removing the pipe from his

102

mouth, he held it at his side as his eyes fastened on mine. "But you're not here to talk about us."

"No," I agreed. "I'm here to talk about your son."

Seth and Clover Richwine exchanged glances. Whatever it was, they were both thinking the same thing. "Seth . . . ?" she pleaded.

"I don't have a son," he answered, laying down his pipe and picking up his Western. "Now I'll thank you to get out of my house."

"He's not from the army, Seth," Clover said. "He's got other reasons for looking for Jack."

He gave her a harsh look. "Then he can look somewhere else besides my house."

"I invited Mr. Ryland in," she said stubbornly. "And he's not leaving until I say so."

He didn't answer, but turned to his Western instead. An uncomfortable silence followed. Then Clover Richwine stood and motioned for me to follow her.

We went as far as the kitchen, where we sat across an oak table from each other. She adjusted her wig, which had slipped to one side, making her head lopsided. "I bet I look foolish, don't I?" she asked.

"You look fine," I said.

She nodded toward the living room where Seth sat. "He'll be in that chair until milking time, then again after supper until he falls asleep watching T.V. I usually don't get more than a blink and a nod from him. Tonight I'll be lucky to get that. But he's not a bad man. It's just that life has sort of soured him, like cream when it curdles from being kept too long. You don't use your sweetness in its time, that's what happens to it."

"You don't look soured on life," I observed.

"That's because I've never given in to it, like Seth has." She smiled at me. I saw a trace of tears in it. "It's beaten me down flat, especially this business about

Jack. But I've tried to hold my ground, and not let it have its way completely."

"You and my Grandmother Ryland," I said. "Life knocked her down a lot of times, but she always managed to get up again."

"Was she a farmwife?"

"Until my grandfather died and left her with four small children to raise. Then she was whatever she needed to be."

"Do you favor her?"

"I've never really thought about it," I said. "She was one of a kind."

She smiled wistfully. "There used to be one of those around here."

"Until Jack left home?"

She sighed, looking away. "He'd changed even before that. He and Seth never got along, ever since Jack was a little fellow. Seth said I carried him too high, that no child was worth all that attention. So since I gave Jack so much of me, Seth didn't give him very much of himself, only the back of his hand whenever Jack got out of line." Placing both of her hands on the table, she glanced from one to the other. "Things didn't get any better between them as Jack got older. Jack hated his father, and Seth could barely stand the sight of him."

"Which is the reason why Jack left home to join the army?" I asked.

"One of the reasons," she said. "I'm ashamed to tell you the other one."

"He got somebody pregnant?"

"A fifteen-year-old tramp." She shook her head in disbelief. "All of the nice girls Jack could have had, and he took up with the likes of her. I tell you, Mr. Ryland. Sometimes I have to wonder just how far from the tree the fruit does fall."

"Sometimes I have to wonder that, too," I agreed. Then I asked, "Have you heard from Jack since he left home for the army?"

"At first every week. He was about as homesick as a boy could get. Then regular, but not as often. Then not at all for the longest time until he showed up here one evening wanting money." She leaned back in her chair to look into the living room to make sure Seth didn't overhear. "Seth was out in the barn milking at the time. Jack must have counted on that, which is why he showed up when he did."

"Did you give him the money?"

"All we had in the house." She lowered her voice. "I told Seth I didn't know what happened to it. Maybe he'd misplaced it somewhere."

"Was there much money involved?"

She didn't answer right away. The remembrance still haunted her. "All our seed money for that year. That's why we started renting this place. We couldn't afford to put out our own crops."

"For want of a nail," I said.

"What's that, Mr. Ryland?"

"Nothing." Looking out the kitchen window, I could see a wellhouse and a woodshed. Like the rest of the farm, both needed repair. "Have you heard from Jack since then?" I asked.

She looked down at her hands, pale and thin like the rest of her.

"Mrs. Richwine, please. It's important. Perhaps some lives have already been lost."

She looked up at me with tears in her eyes. "I know." She excused herself and went upstairs. When she came back down again, she removed a letter from her shoe and handed it to me.

"May I read it?" I asked.

She touched a finger to her lips for silence. I understood.

Dear Mom,

   I just wanted you to know I am all right, so don't you worry, like I know you are. I've made a home for myself up here in the north woods, hunting and trapping and living off the land, like I used to there at home when I was a kid. I have a place way back in the wilderness that used to belong to an old trapper, who gave it up and moved to Florida a few years ago. I like the peace and quiet, but the winters are awful long, especially when the ice starts breaking up in the spring, and while you want to, you can't go nowhere. I have a job guiding for a woman named Patsy Bircher, who owns a lodge up here. It's good money, but it's seasonal, so the rest of the time I have to get by the best I can.

   There's no woman in my life right now, but with a little luck all that might change soon. Of course, no woman can ever take your place, Mom, but a man does have his needs. That is, if he's any man at all, which I definitely am.

   Tell the old man for me that I'll repay that money I borrowed if it's the last thing I do. You might also tell that old sonofabitch for me that I'll hate him until the day I die.

   Take care of yourself, Mom. I love you.

He left the letter unsigned. Putting it back into its envelope, I noted the postmark. It had been stamped in Sand Lake, Minnesota, five years before. "Thank you," I said. "For sharing it with me."

She bit her lip, then turned away so I wouldn't see her cry.

A few minutes later she walked me to the door.

**106**

Seth had coughed himself into a near spasm, then fallen asleep in his chair. When I stepped outside and the screen door banged behind me, I felt immense relief, as though I'd reentered life.

"Thanks for everything," I said. "I know that wasn't easy."

Clover Richwine smiled sadly. "Easier than you think."

"I don't understand."

"Jack's dead, Mr. Ryland. I know it in my bones. So whatever you do to him, you can't hurt him."

Too numb to speak, I could only wait for my voice to return. "Are you sure?"

"As sure as I can be without seeing his body."

"How long has he been dead?"

"Over three years now. It just hit me one day, this terrible sadness. Then I knew it must be Jack."

"You couldn't be mistaken?"

"I could be," she said. "I pray I am. But I don't think so."

On I-94 between Madison and Superior, somewhere around Black River Falls, Wisconsin, the north begins. More needles, fewer notches appear in the leaves as reedy lakes replace fields and farms, and aspens fence the roads. The air becomes a little cleaner, the sky a little bluer, the distance between houses a little farther. Country stores, roadside chapels, and roadside bars sprout like volunteer corn along the highways and byways and in places where even the moose need a map to find their way out again. There's a subtle change in the people, too, a tougher texture to their smiles, a thin sheath of leather upon their faces and over their hearts. Quick to take your dollar, they are sometimes slow to take your hand. For as you travel deeper into the north, into its pure, unbending silence that leaves nothing to chance, you realize that unless you are wolf, eagle, or pine, you are an interloper there. Its ways are not your ways; its will is not your own. You must give the north its due, grant it the respect it demands, and above all, choose your friends as carefully as you choose your character, since either, in a land so harsh and unforgiving, can cost you your life.

I drove all afternoon and into the evening, ate supper in Superior at a downtown diner near the iron ore docks, then crossed the toll bridge into Duluth and continued north on U.S. 53. I passed Virginia, Minnesota, in the dark, and a little over an hour later turned east in Orley, Minnesota, at a sign pointing toward Sand Lake. Slowing to about thirty, I rolled down my window all the way and put Jessie on automatic pilot.

It was a warm, fragrant night, unusually warm for the north that late in the year, and I was alone on the road, surrounded by the smell of balsam and a pine forest as deep as my thoughts. For years I'd had a recurring dream of coming to the north woods to fish, and never making that first cast. In desperation I'd slip in and out of cabins, sneak in and out of boats, do anything and everything to get to the water, only to find myself dry-docked again. As I drove toward Sand Lake without my rod or reel or any of my fishing tackle, the irony didn't escape me.

I came to a fork in the road. A sign pointed left to the Black Bear Lodge; another sign pointed right to the Bumble Bee Resort. I turned left toward the Black Bear Lodge, hitting gravel about two hundred yards down the road. At that same moment I first saw Sand Lake through a break in the trees. A short while later I came to the Black Bear Lodge. It wasn't hard to find. The road ended there.

After parking Jessie under an aspen, I walked

down to the dock to stretch my legs. A crescent moon swam in white ripples upon the water, while in the distance the silhouette of a small island shimmered like a ship moored at sea. Beyond that was only lake, woods, and sky.

Hearing a boat coming full speed down the lake toward me, I cupped my hand over my eyes to try to find it. Whoever drove the boat would have to know Sand Lake well—every rock, point, and reef, then have the courage to put that knowledge to the test. He entered the bay, a black dot growing larger, sped toward the pier to my right until the last instant, then sharply turned the boat and shut off the motor, gliding to a rest against the pier with the bow of the boat nosed out toward the lake better to ride the incoming wake. I was waiting for him to reveal himself when, with catlike speed and sureness, he jumped out of the boat and tied it to the pier in the time it took for his wake to reach shore. Then, before I could follow, he jumped from the pier and disappeared into the shadows.

After washing my face in the lake, I walked to where his boat was tied and knelt at the edge of the pier to examine it. *Kawoosh!* A rock hit the water behind me. It sounded as though the sky had fallen. I didn't have a chance to move before its splash rained down on me.

I went up into the pines to investigate, saw nothing but the soft scattered lights of Black Bear's cabins. The night, warm all the way in to Sand Lake, turned suddenly cool. I shivered. The north always found a way to give me the chills.

# 8

Cramped and cold, I crawled out of Jessie at dawn and walked down to the dock in the hope of intercepting the man who had landed in the night. During the night, a short while after I had bedded down in Jessie's backseat, I'd heard someone walking in the gravel behind me and raised myself up to see who it was. But he'd moved on into the shadows. Soon after that I heard a boat motor fire, and someone left at idle speed.

So it didn't surprise me in the morning to discover the boat was gone. After searching the dock and along the shore without finding it, I washed my hands and face in the lake, made a halfhearted attempt to unsnarl my hair, and walked back up to where Jessie was parked. There I took a moment to look around.

Black Bear Lodge sat in the woods a hundred yards above me. Nearer the shoreline, but still in the woods, sat a row of rental cabins as plain and spare as the lodge itself. At the water's edge, where the road ended in a ramp, stood a large corrugated metal building that smelled like fish and fuel oil. A short way up the hill from it a small frame building served as a bar, grocery store, bait shop, and coffee shop all in one. The hub of Black Bear's wheel, it was the only place showing any life on that quiet, deceptively serene Sunday morning.

Inside the coffee shop I took a seat at the counter near the window, where I could watch the sun rise across the lake. The woman behind the counter had a round face, brown medium-length hair, straight-cut bangs, and a freshly scrubbed I'm-all-business look. She wore jeans, hiking shoes, and a tan cotton shirt, and was filling saltshakers when she could get the salt to pour. From the back, in well-filled jeans and with her bobbed hair, she looked like a ripe sixteen-year-old. From the front, deep weather lines showing in her face, reserve and resolve showing in her not so soft brown eyes, she looked older, closer to forty. From any angle she looked like a woman who could take care of herself.

"What'll it be?" she asked.

"Coffee, toast, two eggs over easy, and hash browns, if they don't come from a box," I said.

"They do," she answered.

"Then forget the hash browns." To me, box hash browns tasted like cardboard.

While she went into the kitchen to fix my order, I took a tour of the coffee shop. It had a log floor, knotty pine paneling, the obligatory fish mounted on the wall above the door, and the obligatory beer clock mounted on the wall above the cooler. On the other side of the room the bait shop offered a small selection of over-priced lures and fishing tackle, fresh and frozen min-nows, and night crawlers for two dollars a dozen. High on everything but choices, it was designed with the tourist in mind.

On my way back to the counter I stopped to admire a pencil drawing that depicted with a grouse, a star, and a pine the dark blue silence of a north winter night. The longer I looked, the more I liked it. I wished it were hanging in my office at home.

"How much?" I asked the woman as she came out of the kitchen.

"It's not for sale." She resented my even asking.

"I didn't think so. Do you know the name of the artist?"

"It doesn't matter," she said coldly. "He's dead."

"I'm sorry to hear that," I said. "I would have liked to have seen some of his other work."

She went back into the kitchen and returned with my order, setting it down in front of me. "You're a new face around here," she observed.

"I'm a new everything around here," I answered. "Could I have some cream for my coffee, please?" She brought me a quart of milk from the cooler. I poured some into my coffee and handed the carton back to her. "Thanks."

"You come in last night?" she asked with a persistent air.

"More like early this morning," I said between bites.

"Did you check in?"

"No. Was I supposed to?"

She gave me a look not intended to warm my heart. "You're a guest, aren't you?" she asked.

I got the message. Guests were welcome at the Black Bear Lodge, not necessarily so for everyone else. "No. I'm not a guest. I'm looking for someone named Patsy Bircher."

"Then you found her." Not warm to begin with, the temperature in there took a nosedive.

"Lucky me."

"So what are you selling?" she demanded.

"Nothing. Do you mind if I eat before my eggs get cold? I hate to talk with my mouth full." I also didn't like her attitude, which bordered on surly.

Returning to the kitchen, she soon came out again, scanned Sand Lake and the surrounding shoreline, and filled a couple more saltshakers. She apparently had more on her mind than guests that morning. Meanwhile I finished my breakfast and asked for a refill on the coffee. She brought the milk without my asking for it. I heard a crackle and then a man's voice. Another man answered. The voices came from the C.B. on top of the cooler.

Patsy Bircher closely monitored the conversation, hanging on every word, as if she were afraid Jack might come jumping out of the box. Then she turned to me. "Are you through?" she asked.

"Yes."

She took my plate and silverware into the kitchen. I held onto my coffee cup to make sure she didn't take that. "So," she said abruptly on her return, "what do you want with me? And make it short, because in about fifteen minutes this place is going to start filling up."

For the first time I saw activity around the dock. Boats were being loaded, gas tanks filled, fishing tackle checked and rechecked, as guides and guests alike prepared for the day's fishing. But one early-riser had the jump on everyone else. He suddenly appeared from around a bend in the shoreline, dipped in toward the dock, and expertly guided his boat alongside it, where he began to fill up with gas. I could tell by the way he moved, casually, almost insolently, jumping from boat to dock with no thought for his safety, that it was the same man I'd seen in the night. I walked to the window for a better look at him, but he was too far away to make out. I noticed Patsy Bircher watching him, too.

"Who's that?" I asked.

"I don't know who it is."

But her eyes stayed on the man the entire time he was at the dock, then on the silver V of his boat as it sped up Sand Lake. I couldn't read what was in her eyes. Not love, yet not hate either. Longing perhaps. Or irony. In any case, nothing that brought a smile. "Okay," she said, turning to me, "you're finished eating now. So who are you? What are you doing here? And, I repeat, what do you want with me?"

I sat back down to drink the rest of my coffee. "My name is Garth Ryland," I said. "I'm looking for John Knight."

At the sound of his name her eyes darted from me to Sand Lake, then back to me again. "Why are you looking for John Knight, and what makes you think I know where he is?"

Reaching inside my shirt, I took out the letter that Jack Richwine, alias John Knight, had written his mother. She'd given it to me on my promise that I'd return it to her when I was through with it.

I took the letter out of the envelope and laid it on the counter in front of Patsy Bircher, where she would have to read it. "It's not signed," she said when she finished.

"Does it have to be?"

She took a seat with her back to me at the counter, staring out across Sand Lake, searching for the wake of the man who'd left Black Bear waters a few minutes earlier. "When did John write that?" she asked.

"Five years ago."

She wore a look of irony that I understood only too well. "Has it been that long? It seems only yesterday . . ." She stopped, realizing where she was and to whom she was talking.

"Only yesterday what?" I asked.

Tears ran down her cheeks as she spun around to face me. "Damn you," she said. "I haven't seen John Knight for four years. Why bring him up to me now?"

I told her why. She shook her head when I finished. Not knowing whether I'd hit a bull's-eye or not, I asked, "Why don't you believe me?"

"It doesn't matter," she answered, "whether I believe you or not. I don't know where John Knight is. Like I told you before, I haven't seen him in four years."

Far to the north a white dot of wake appeared momentarily, then disappeared again. "What about the man in that boat? Couldn't he be John Knight?"

"I told you. I've never seen that man before."

"You're sure?"

Her eyes snapped as she said "I'm sure."

I showed her the photograph of Devin and Helen LeMay on their wedding day. "What about these two people? Have you ever seen either one of them?"

Studying the people in the photograph, she looked as though she recognized them.

"Well?" I said when she didn't answer.

"The man looks vaguely familiar," she said, measuring her words. "I think he stayed over at the Bumble Bee a few years back."

"And the woman?"

She dropped the photograph on the counter. I got the feeling that if I hadn't been there, she would have torn it in two. "Mr. Ryland, you've wasted enough of my time for one day."

"If I come back later?"

**115**

She rose from the counter. "No. Two hours from now I'll be knee-deep in details because this place won't run itself. Then this afternoon I'm flying a party of four over to Lac LaCroix. Then tonight is my cook's night off, so I have to help at the lodge. After that I come back here to finish my day."

I stood, drinking the rest of my coffee. "Thanks for breakfast. It was good."

"Where are you going?" she asked.

"I thought you were trying to get rid of me."

"You know what I mean."

I pointed to an imaginary dot on Sand Lake. "I'm going after the man in that boat."

"Not in one of my boats, you aren't."

"There's more than one boatkeeper on Sand Lake," I said, remembering the sign advertising the Bumble Bee Resort.

She bristled. "Good luck in finding one." She walked through the door of the kitchen and didn't come back out. I laid a five-dollar bill on the counter and left.

A walk along the shore of Sand Lake told me I wouldn't find any help there. What Patsy Bircher didn't own included the lake, sky, and a couple of private cabins that had no boats for rent. Returning to the coffee shop, I found a pay phone outside and made a credit card call home.

"Garth? Where are you?" Ruth said. She almost sounded glad to hear from me.

"Sand Lake, Minnesota," I said. "Tell Rupert I've tracked John Knight this far, and I'm going into the bush after him as soon as I can find a boat."

"Is that wise?" she asked.

"Probably not, since it's his territory, not mine. But in any case I won't be home by tomorrow, I'm sure. So you'd better get the ball rolling on the *Oakalla Reporter*."

Dead silence from her end.

"Ruth, are you still there?"

"I'm still here," she said. "But what do I know about putting out a newspaper?"

"You said you were editor of your high school yearbook." Opening the coin return, I found a quarter there.

"That was over a hundred years ago," she answered. "I've slept since then."

I pocketed the quarter. Maybe it would bring me luck. "I have confidence in you, Ruth," I said. "Now I've got to go."

"Shouldn't you wait for help?" she asked.

"I don't see any on the way," I said as I hung up.

The last I saw of Patsy Bircher, she stood at the window of the coffee shop watching for me. I waved as I drove by, but she didn't wave back. When I reached the Y in the road I'd passed in the night, I turned east toward the Bumble Bee Resort. I wasn't encouraged.

Faded, his wings beaten to nubs, the bee painted on the sign had made his maiden flight years ago. The farther I went along the washboard road leading to the Bumble Bee Resort, the deeper my doubts grew, as the trees closed in like pickets, and the road narrowed between them. Glancing up at the sky, all but obscured by the trees, I saw a web of cirrus hanging in the east ahead of me. Too faint even to cast a shadow, it soon eclipsed the sun, darkening the woods, and, like a half-heard whisper, left me uneasy about what might come. Then I broke into a clearing and saw the sparkle of Sand Lake ahead. Like one seeing a familiar face after a night among strangers, I smiled in greeting.

In the clearing an old green GMC pickup was parked in front of a two-story log building. Since its tires were all up and its hood was down, I guessed it still ran.

"Make me an offer," someone said, as I climbed out of Jessie. A gnarled, bony wisp of a man whose hair hung in white tufts from beneath his red corduroy cap leaned on a cane in the doorway of the building.

"A hundred dollars," I said.

"One fifty and it's yours."

"Too much," I said. "Besides, I've got a car."

He squinted, using his free hand to shield his eyes from the sun. "Not much of one," he said, "by the looks of it. But throw in a sawbuck, and I'll trade you even."

I was tempted, but if nothing else, I was loyal. Besides, he had no idea what he'd be in for. "Thanks anyway. But I'll hang on to her for a while yet."

"Anything else I might do you out of?" he asked.

"You never know."

"Well, then come on in."

He went inside while I climbed the steps to the porch. Some soft, others rotten, the steps gave underfoot like March ice, but once I made it to the porch, the view was magnificent. Lake, tree, and sky stretched out to the north as far as I could see, until somewhere on the far horizon, like eye, dream, and mind, they merged as one. About a hundred yards away a neat row of well-made cabins sat tucked in the woods along the shore; beneath me, the frame of a yellow Lawnboy sat rusting among the heather. I guessed that once upon a time, before time clipped his wings, the Bumble Bee was *the* resort on Sand Lake.

I went inside the building. Discovering it was a fully stocked general store, I couldn't hide my surprise. "They don't eat anything," the old man said, referring to the shelves of canned goods.

"Do you ever sell anything?" I blew the dust off a can of tomato soup. A few days earlier I'd done the same thing in John Knight's house along Lost Road. But even though the two actions were the same, the feel of the house and of the old man's store were as different as night and day.

"Once in a while a tourist will get lost and wander in here," he said in answer to my question. "But I'm not likely ever to see him again."

"Then how do you stay in business?" From the depth of the dust covering everything, it looked as though nothing much had moved in there lately.

He smiled at me. He had the quick bright eyes of a child. "The how ain't hard. I've already bought the stuff; I might as well try to sell it. It's the why you're asking."

Together we watched a spider ride a strand of silk down from the ceiling, then drop and run once it hit the counter. "Okay, why do you stay in business?" I asked.

He swung at the spider with his cane, but missed. "There's nothing else to do," he said. "Guess I could fish, but I've caught all I want to out of this lake. I could guide, but I'm getting a little old to be helping fat women in and out of boats. I could trap, but that's a fool's job. So I sit in here all day and kill bugs."

"What about in winter?"

He took bead on an ant crossing the counter. "I go south."

"How far south?"

"Duluth. I've got family there. What's left of it." The cane smacked against the counter, flipping the ant to the floor, but the ant quickly righted itself and wobbled away.

The old man wore a wedding band. But like everything else there at the Bumble Bee, it had worn thin. "Are you married?"

"Was. She died about five years ago." He looked at

119

his watch. "Four years, ninety-three days, and twelve hours to be exact. Blood vessel broke in her brain. That's the way the doctor explained it to me. Said there was nothing nobody could do. We were married fifty-two years," he said, sitting back in his chair. "At the most I regretted five of them."

"I was married ten years. At the least I regretted nine of them." I didn't count the year my son was born.

But he wasn't listening. He closed his eyes and went on talking. "Thirty-one and Thirty-two, those were the hardest. By that time the stardust had worn off and we'd realized what we'd done. Here I was married to a mama's girl who cried at the drop of a hat and here she was married to a dreamer who didn't have a pot to pee in and no prospect of getting one. Hammered out a marriage in spite of ourselves. Wasn't a question of love. First we had to learn how to live with each other. Love, at least the kind that takes, didn't come along until a lot later."

"How much later?" I asked. Because no matter how much I loved Diana and she loved me, it wasn't enough to keep her in Oakalla.

"Hard to say. I just know it was there over the years or we never would've survived. Lost one of our three sons—to the lake. Had hard times and good times. But all in all they averaged out." Ignoring an ant that had wandered into range, he laid his cane on the counter. "But that's not why you're here, is it, to hear my life story?"

"No. I came to rent a boat."

"Why?"

"I'm looking for someone."

"Who?" He wouldn't let me off that easily.

I decided I'd get a lot farther if I told him the truth. "John Knight. Have you seen him lately?"

He perked up, like an old fox catching a familiar scent. "Winter Knight, you say? Is he back on Sand Lake?"

"That depends," I said, telling my heart not to race. "Who's Winter Knight?"

"Winter Knight is a local," he said. "He used to live by himself up on Wild Horse Lake until he took off about three or four years ago and just dropped off the edge of the world. In fact I've still got that big boat of his in storage here. What's left of it. Three winters ago the snow got so deep on top of my storage building it collapsed the roof and crushed nearly everything in it." Raising his cane, he lashed out at an ant, narrowly missing it. "That about put me out of the boat business."

For the first time since I'd started the search for John Knight, I felt I was close to finding him. That thought alone made me impatient. "But have you seen him recently?" I asked.

He shook his head. "Not him in the flesh. Just signs of him, that's all. Like that black truck of his parked out near the garbage dump. And other locals saying that it looked like he might be building something up on Wild Horse Lake."

I laid the photograph of Devin and Helen LeMay in front of him. "Have you seen either one of these two people?"

He picked up the photograph and studied it. As he did, a smile of recognition crossed his face. "She is a beauty, isn't she?"

"I've heard she is. I've never seen her."

His smile deepened. "Then you've missed something." He clicked his tongue in admiration. "No wonder Winter never had a chance."

"In what way?"

121

He sighed, picking up his cane to threaten an ant, then putting it back down again. "I don't think it was one any more than the other. They just clicked, that's all, like people do sometimes. Neither one of them had the willpower, or even the good sense, to fight it." He shook his head sadly, ignoring an ant that seemed intent on provoking him. "It was her husband, that young college professor, who I felt sorry for. Here he'd come up on his honeymoon and asked for the very same cabin where he and his grandmother used to stay when he was a boy, and that's the way things turned out."

"Devin LeMay had been up here before?" I asked.

"Back in the fifties he and his grandmother used to come up every year and stay in cabin number one." He smiled as he recalled them. "I never saw two people of different generations get on so well. They were always together, whether out on the lake fishing, or picking blueberries, or sneaking down to the dump to watch the bears." His smile faded. "That all ended, though, when they brought the boy's mother along one year. She wouldn't let him get more than two steps away from the cabin before she'd call him back again. That was the beginning of the end of it. After a couple more years of putting up with that, it just wasn't worth it to any of them to come back. Though, the grandmother did make one appearance by herself. But without the boy along she took no pleasure in it, and didn't even bother to stay out the week, if I remember right."

"Are you sure it was the fifties?" I asked, remembering that Devin LeMay was only thirty-four.

"Fifties or sixties, somewhere in there," he said. "We hadn't had this place all that long, I know that. If Anna were here, she could tell you. She never forgot a name or a date."

122

"Anna?"

"My late wife."

In the silence that followed I counted seven ants and two spiders crawling across the counter at once. But the old man made no move toward any of them.

"Have you seen Devin LeMay lately?" I asked.

He nodded. "He stopped by here a couple weeks ago and wanted to know if cabin number one was vacant. I said they were all vacant and he could have his pick, stay a week or a month, whatever he liked. He said thanks, but he'd only be staying the night. There was someone he wanted to show cabin number one."

I already knew who that someone was. Taking a photograph of Diana from my wallet, I handed it to him. "Is she the one?" I asked.

"Could be," he answered. "She was in the car the whole time. I only saw her wave at me."

"Did you see either her or Devin LeMay again?"

"No. They were gone by the time I got up." A shadow drifted across Sand Lake, which was dead calm, not a ripple showing. "But the car's still here."

"Where?" I didn't recall seeing it anywhere.

"It'll be easier to show you."

A few minutes later he led me along a path to the edge of a dump where John Knight's black short-bed pickup was parked. Parked beside it was Devin LeMay's silver Porsche. Something within me recoiled at the sight of it, and I remembered feeling the same on the night I first saw it parked outside of Diana's apartment. Up until then I hadn't had to face the fact that Diana had been there with Devin LeMay.

"You recognize the car?" the old man asked.

"Yes. It looks like Devin LeMay's."

"I thought so, too."

A black bear feeding at the dump caught our scent

and ran off into the woods. We could hear it crash through the underbrush all the way to the shore of Sand Lake. Then the woods fell silent again.

"Did you hear their car leave in the night?" I asked.

"No. But I sleep pretty sound once I get around to it." He pointed his cane at a whiskey jack who had begun hurling insults in our direction. "But I did think I heard a boat toward morning."

"Going or coming?"

"Going, I think."

The whiskey jack suddenly took flight. The silence that followed seemed deeper than before. "You say you know where John Knight lives?"

"I know where he used to live," he answered.

Back at the store he found a map of the region and showed me Wild Horse Lake. I counted at least twelve miles between the Bumble Bee Resort and there, which was too far to paddle round-trip in one day. "Do you have a boat and motor I could rent?" I asked.

"Nope. I sold my last good one just the other day. But you can borrow my fishing rig, if you promise to bring it back in one piece."

"If I come back in one piece, it'll come back in one piece."

"That's what I meant."

Within the hour I sat in his outfit, a fourteen-foot-square–stern Grummon canoe with an ancient three-horse Johnson outboard motor on the back. I left my wool shirt and stocking cap in Jessie, but took along my rain suit, compass, and the sack lunch the old man had packed for me. I also had a map of Sand Lake, a two-gallon can of gas, a funnel for the gas, and a canoe paddle in case I needed it.

"Here." He handed me a small green toolbox.

"There's some pliers, plugs, and extra shear pins inside. Where you're going, you might need them."

"Anything else I might need?"

He handed me a seat cushion that doubled as a life preserver. "Just don't try to wear it on your back if you go over."

"Thanks," I said. "I won't."

Balanced on his cane, he began to untie me from the pier. "I don't know how familiar you are with the north country, but it's my guess you've been up here before, so I won't clutter your mind with a lot of advice you won't take or don't need. Just remember to look for rocks even where they aren't supposed to be and don't shave any points too close. Other than that you're on your own." He scanned the sky with concern. "One other thing," he said, as his eyes swept Sand Lake, a flawless blue mirror. "This lake can turn inside out in a hurry. So don't be on the water if a storm hits."

I primed the choke and pulled on the starter cord. The Johnson fired on the first pull. "John Knight," I said. "I've never seen him, only had him described to me. What does he look like?"

"He's about your height, say six feet. Slender build, but all sinew and bone. Black hair and bushy black beard that make him look older than he is. Mirror eyes," he added as an afterthought.

"Mirror eyes?"

"He can see out, but you can't always see in." He scratched his chin thoughtfully. "Come to think of it, maybe that's where the name Winter came from. Or the fact that he'll see you long before you see him, and come rushing in like a cold wind."

"Like the wind off a frozen lake?" I asked.

"Something like that," he said. "At least the effect's the same." He threw the tie rope into the canoe, then, steadying himself with his cane, reached down to shake my hand. "Take care of yourself," he said.

"Thanks. I'll try to." I pushed away from the pier, put the Johnson in forward gear, and took off for Wild Horse Lake.

# 9

$I$ had Sand Lake to myself. Here and there along the shore and on most of the larger islands that dotted it, I could see boats and cabins and an occasional strand of smoke, but no boaters and no fishermen. I liked the solitude. I liked Sand Lake, the lay of the land and the smell of the pines, the warmth of the sun and the blue of the sky. I liked the way the motor purred like a contented cat, the feathery feel of the canoe as it skimmed the water. I had never felt more alive than right there, right then. And never closer to death.

I came to the narrows that was the halfway point between the Bumble Bee Resort and Wild Horse Bay. Granite cliffs grew straight up out of the water like stalagmites on both sides of the narrows, blocking the sun. Suddenly I went from sunlight to shadow. Looking down into the still black water, it seemed fathomless, hiding in its black depths the bones of Iroquois, Voyageurs, and loggers alike. Looking up, I saw a bald eagle sitting straight atop a dead pine. He didn't look down at me, move one feather of acknowledgment. As I passed through the narrows, going from shadow to sunlight again, I felt I'd passed the point of no return and couldn't turn back even if I wanted to.

About a mile beyond the narrows I found a small sand beach that appeared a good place to land. I shut off the motor, lifted the prop out of the water, and paddled the rest of the way in. I was glad I took the precaution. As the old man warned, there were rocks where there shouldn't be, rocks I hadn't seen. Any one of them could have broken the prop.

Pulling the canoe snugly up onto the sand beach, I sat on a boulder in the sunlight and ate the lunch the old man had packed for me. It included a peanut butter and jelly sandwich, an orange, a dill pickle, and a Snickers for dessert. Then I knelt and drank out of the lake, something I'd done many times in the north. It was almost mandated, to prove that somewhere on this once-green earth nothing had really changed.

Over thirty years before, on my first fishing trip to the north, my family and I had stopped for a shore lunch in a small bay much like the one where I was. I put on a life jacket and began to paddle around the bay. Several yards from shore, where there should have been nothing but water, something sharp scraped my stomach as I swam over it. It didn't draw blood. It just left a long white scratch on my skin, as my first reminder never to take the north for granted.

Small white threads had wormed their way into the blue of the sky. There on the shore, without the lake to stir it, the air felt heavy and close. I filled the Johnson with gas and went on. Five miles later I approached what on the map appeared to be Wild Horse Bay.

Several small islands, some no more than piles of broken rock, guarded the entrance to the bay, revealing no clear channel inside. The safest route was a circle far to the west around the islands to come into the bay from the north. But since I was approaching from the south, following the east shoreline, the quickest route led straight ahead.

Idling the motor, I scanned the water for rocks. Low and broken, the east shoreline came to a sharp point several yards ahead. Straight out from the point, about two hundred yards into the bay, sat an island, followed by several other islands in a row. Islands in a row usually meant an interconnecting reef.

I shut off the motor and began to paddle, aiming halfway between the point and the first island. Though I expected the reef, it still took my breath away. Yellow and massive, pocked with small craters like acne scars, it lay just beneath the surface, like some primordial sea serpent awaiting its next victim. I stopped paddling and drifted, afraid one of the craters would suck the paddle into its rock jaws and snap it off, then sighed in relief when the water turned green, then blue again.

Wild Horse Bay was the mouth of the Wild Horse River. Wild Horse Lake was the source of the river about three miles upstream. John Knight lived somewhere on Wild Horse Lake. But Wild Horse River couldn't make up its mind just where it wanted to go. Small granite bluffs marked its mouth, but these gave way to coots and mallards, wild rice and lily pads, as the river widened and began to meander. A narrow twisting path between the weeds, the channel kept doubling back upon itself, like a snake winding its way through the underbrush.

About two miles in I shut off the motor, wanting to go quietly from there on—to match the day, which had stopped moving altogether. I began to sweat. The paddle slid back and forth in my hands as I twisted along the channel of Wild Horse River, small pike darting in and out of the weeds ahead of me. On bottom I saw snags and beaver cuttings, and an occasional log that Paul Bunyan and Babe had lost a century before, then a can, a bottle, and a shiny piece of tinfoil—newer, smaller remnants of civilization.

I came around a tight bend, saw something gray at the edge of the water, and stopped paddling. The wolf, if that's what it was, whirled and disappeared into the underbrush, leaving me only the impression I had seen something grand and rare. I paddled on, ever more aware that I was an interloper in a land that, by reputation and design, took care of its own.

The river narrowed and blackened as I approached an earthen dam. The old man at the Bumble Bee had said to expect the dam. Lumberjacks had built it before he was born to raise the river level high enough to float their logs out of Wild Horse Lake.

I found some limbs and small logs, most of them beaver cuttings, and placed these at four-foot intervals up and down the short steep portage leading around the dam. Then I rolled the canoe up and over the portage. Waiting for me on the other side was a narrow rock valley and a growing swarm of deerflies that all tried to bite me at once. Even though the canoe took only a few inches of draft, I couldn't paddle it once I got it back into the water. I had to walk and drag it most of the way to Wild Horse Lake, three hundred yards beyond the dam. Biting every step of the way, the deerflies followed me. Only when I reached open water and could paddle again did I leave some of them behind.

I glanced at the sky, half expecting what I saw. An

eerie blue—a shade I hadn't seen before—it seemed to congeal, darkening and thickening like blue blood. More green than blue, the lake almost matched the sky, and gave me the sensation of gliding over green glass. I saw a chimney, then the outline of a cabin. I paddled on, entering a small shallow bay that had weeds growing almost to the end of John Knight's pier. Roughly made out of hard-hewn planks and timbers, scarred, battered, and weathered nearly white, the pier seemed as durable as the north itself. Seeing no boat or canoe or anything else on shore that would tell me John Knight was home, or that he'd ever been home in the past three years, I paddled on in and dragged the canoe up on the sand beside the pier. I took a long time deciding what I wanted to do next. Finally I went on up the hill.

Square and solid, with only two small windows, no porch front or back, and one door on the south side, John Knight's cabin sat on a foundation of solid bedrock high above Wild Horse Lake. A rusty double-bladed ax leaned against a stack of firewood at one end of the cabin, while a stone chimney anchored the other end. Three small outbuildings, each progressively larger, led up into the woods. One, the privy, I knew too well, from my early days on Grandmother's farm. I remembered how it had shone with bright malice on a clear winter's night. The second outbuilding appeared to be a toolshed and workshop. The third, long, low, and windowless, darker than the others, looked like a beached whale. I guessed it was John Knight's trapping shed, where he skinned the animals, then stretched the pelts and hung them up to dry. I decided to try the cabin first.

Dim and cool inside, the cabin smelled faintly of must and smoke. Directly in front of me, black with the soot of a thousand fires, a huge stone fireplace yawned like the mouth of a cave. Above the hearth, securely resting on a rack of moose antlers, was a .300 Winchester Magnum with a 2½X Weaver scope mounted on it. Both rifle and scope were dust-covered and flecked with rust.

I opened the breech and found no cartridge inside. Neither did I find any lying on top of the mantel. After wiping both lenses clean with my shirt, I used the scope to scan Wild Horse Lake, but didn't see John Knight anywhere about.

John Knight's bed sat against the west wall across the room from the fireplace. An iron bed covered with a thick blue patchwork quilt and several wool blankets, it reminded me of my bed at Grandmother Ryland's. Diana's suitcase and duffel bag, along with those of Devin LeMay, sat open on top of it. But though the suitcases were open, their contents looked untouched, and this told me more than I wanted to know.

Lifting Diana's silk nightgown from her suitcase, I pressed it against my face. A hint of her perfume clung to it, made the lump in my throat grow larger. I couldn't believe I might never hold her again, feel her skin against mine. I didn't care about New Mexico or what it might bring. I just wanted one more night with her—to take her in my arms and love her one last time.

Outside, the sky was a pale green, fading to yellow. Somewhere out on Wild Horse Lake a loon laughed, wildly, crazily, eerily, as only a loon can laugh. A beaver's tail smacked the water like a rifle's report. I flinched from the sound, made larger by the stillness of the day.

Stopping at each outbuilding in turn, I came to the skinning shed. It looked far newer than the other buildings and out of place among them. Unlike the privy and the workshop, both square honest buildings that did not hide what they were, the skinning shed, built long and low to the ground with no windows to see in or out, seemed surreptitious, almost serpentine the way it lay concealed in the underbrush.

A pair of waxed snowshoes and a well-oiled bear trap hung together on the wall beside the door, like ornaments rather than tools of the north. Nailed above the door, the head of a large pike had hung there just long enough to rot. Flies swarmed around its mouth, crawled in and out of the holes where its eyes had been. It seemed a warning—like the skull and crossbones of the Jolly Roger—that death waited within.

I lifted the heavy wooden bar that fastened the door. The door swung slowly out at me, followed by a putrid breath of air. Before me, there on the dirt floor, maggots swam in a bucket of fish guts. For a moment I couldn't breathe. I felt as though I'd interrupted some obscene ritual and would be damned for my insolence.

After carrying the bucket of fish guts into the woods, I returned to stand at the threshold of the skinning shed. Something held me back—the feeling of impending doom that had followed me ever since I left the old man's dock at the Bumble Bee Resort. I couldn't shake it no matter what. And in its insistence, its bone-deep, gut-grabbing fear, it denied the theory of mind over matter.

I took a step inside the skinning shed. Staring into its blackness as the stench swirled around me gathering a vortex of flies, I felt weak and dizzy, as if I were staring into a black whirlpool. Then a sudden gust of wind that came out of nowhere caught the door and slammed it behind me. I heard the bar fall into place and knew I was trapped.

Momentary panic overcame me as I rushed toward the door, throwing my shoulder against it. Nothing happened. The door didn't give. I didn't bounce backward. We stood shoulder to door, as in an embrace.

Leaves fluttered overhead. Flies swarmed against the door, wanting out. A tree creaked, a limb fell, a loon laughed.

I tried again to budge the door and again got nowhere. It seemed as solid as the walls of the building itself. Looking for another way out, I found it at the far end of the trapping shed, where the head of an old broadax lay upon a fresh pile of pine chips. The broadax had been used by someone else to chop his way out through a hole that was barely big enough for me.

Once free outside, I took one look at the sky and ran down the hill toward the canoe. Prudence said to stay there, because John Knight's cabin would be safer than the open water, but I couldn't make myself listen. I heard a stronger voice saying, Unless you leave Wild Horse Lake at once, you will die there. It didn't remind me of my love for Diana. It didn't say tomorrow is another day. It simply drove me, as a torrent drives a leaf, in a frenzy to escape.

I had put John Knight's cabin well behind me by the time I was in the canoe and racing toward the river. I heard the motor sputter, wanting gas. With no hope of getting to shore as I watched the lilt of the waves increasing, and pushing me ever closer to a humpbacked reef, I spilled more gas than I poured. A rainbow slick spread out behind the boat and rode the waves into the reef. I had no idea of how much gas I'd gotten into the motor—enough, I hoped, to get me out of there.

The river turned as black as the sky. With its rocks and snags hidden beneath a wind-wrinkled surface, it became the enemy, the gauntlet I had to run if I wanted to escape from Wild Horse Lake. I ran it well. I motored

134

as far as I dared without ticking a single rock, but then I came to the rock gorge.

Emptying the canoe, I unfastened the motor and carried it, the gas can, and paddle to the other side of the portage. Then I shouldered the canoe and started up the rock gorge, fell, regained my balance, and fell again, landing heavily on a rock. I couldn't get up. My arms and legs were dead. My whole body shook with fatigue. I couldn't make myself crawl over another rock. But as I sat there in the water, watching the blood seep out from the scrape in my leg, I once again felt the overriding fear of death that had driven me away from John Knight's out into the storm. It gave me the strength to haul the canoe out of the rock gorge and up and over the portage.

The wind rose as the river began to widen. A gust found a seam in the trees and swooped down on me, caught the canoe broadside, and sent it skidding across the water into the weeds. The prop fouled, churning the water like an eggbeater but getting the boat nowhere. I shut off the motor and raised it to unwrap the weeds from around the propeller. In the lull that followed I thought I heard the whine of another motor. Then the sound was lost as the wind began to whip the trees once more. I glanced at the sky. Still darkening like a deep bruise, it had turned a reddish purple where sudden gray flowers bloomed. I'd never seen it look any worse. It looked like the end of the world.

I reached Wild Horse Bay, leaving the river behind. Starting south across the bay, I hoped to find a safe place to land where I could wait out the storm. But I underestimated the wind and the waves. A wave I saw coming but couldn't avoid broke over the bow and rocked the canoe, nearly tipping me from the seat. From

135

then on I knelt in the bottom of the canoe and drove from there.

On Wild Horse Bay, somewhat protected by the wind, the waves had reached a height of two feet and more. Out on the main body of Sand Lake, where the wind had free rein, there was no such thing as a wave. All froth and fury, one white sheet of hell rolled in mass from north to south down the lake.

Glancing back, I thought of returning to the shelter of the Wild Horse River. But another boat had just cleared the river and come into the bay. The boat rode high in the water as it drove straight toward me. I thought I recognized it. It looked like the same boat and driver I'd seen at the Black Bear Lodge.

The boat began to close quickly the distance between us. I remembered, when it had been tied to Black Bear's pier, how the motor had looked too large for the boat. I remembered thinking how even on a calm day, with the motor at full throttle, you'd be riding the envelope between thrill and eternity. Hearing the waves slap its bow as it bore down on me at full speed, I guessed the driver knew the danger but chose to ignore it.

I shielded my eyes against the first burst of rain and aimed for the calmest patch of water I could find, forgetting all about the reef until I saw a wave break ominously on its broad back. I killed the motor, but the wind drove me onto the reef before I could raise the prop. I hit with a jolt and hung there as the other boat kept right on coming. The fool! These were his waters. Didn't he know what lay just ahead?

Rocking the canoe at the same time that I jerked on the motor, I freed the motor momentarily, only to have the wind drive the canoe deeper onto the reef. I jumped out of the canoe, lifted the stern, motor and all, and began dragging the canoe backward across the reef. Falling, I banged both knees, got up, fell again. The other boat meanwhile had passed the point of no return. His eyes fixed on me, his arms a frozen U, bound to the steering wheel like a mannequin's, the driver had seen his mistake and conceded his death.

"Jump!" I yelled above the storm.

He jumped. The boat hit the reef and stopped cold. I smelled gasoline, saw the first spark of a fire, and knew what was about to happen. With a surge of strength I didn't know I had, perhaps would never have again, I wrestled the canoe loose from the reef and began to run with it. I went off the other side of the reef, lost my grip, found it again, and hung there momentarily. Then my foot struck a boulder that I used to climb back into the canoe. At that same instant the boat exploded, raining fire all around me.

# 10

"Where's Diana?" was the first question I asked Devin LeMay.

I'd pulled him unconscious onto the reef, pumped the water out of him, found us some shelter on the east shore of Sand Lake, and waited out the storm. Lying there on a bed of pine needles, Devin LeMay looked even younger and smaller than I remembered him. Slightly built, white-skinned, red-haired, and freckled, he looked as though he should be taking college courses instead of teaching them. That was after I recovered from the shock of recognition. I had fully expected to pull John Knight from the lake.

Devin LeMay opened his eyes a little, then wider when he got a good look at me. He was as surprised to see me as I had been to see him. "You're Garth," he said groggily.

138

"Yes, I am," I said, then repeated, "Where's Diana?"

He shook his head, trying to rise. But the effort was too much for him. He had to lie back down again. "I don't know where she is. I've been searching for her for the last I don't know how many days."

"In whose boat?"

His eyes glazed over momentarily. The question seemed too large for him to comprehend. "My boat, of course. John asked me to bring it along."

"I don't remember seeing a trailer behind your car."

"It's in the weeds there at the dump. John said we'd better hide it, or someone might steal it." Again he tried to rise. That time he made it. "Is the storm over?" he asked.

"Just about. But we probably should wait for the lake to settle down before we start back."

He smiled at me, wanting a smile in return. He reminded me of a beagle pup who, on the strength of his effusion alone, could wiggle his way into your heart. "Thank you for pulling me out of the lake," he said. "I don't know what got into me." Then he corrected himself. "No. That's not true. I know very well what got into me. I thought you were John Knight."

"You intended to kill him?" If not, he could have fooled me.

"I intended to capture him," he answered. "But something snapped in me out there on Wild Horse Bay." His eyes widened at the horror of it. "I lost control of both my aim and myself."

"In what order?"

He glanced away. "I'd rather not say."

"I think that under the circumstances you can probably forgive yourself."

His face darkened. "I wish I could."

Sand Lake began to calm. Only an occasional whitecap flecked the otherwise black swell of water. Then the sun broke through.

"I knew I should never have brought Diana up here," said Devin LeMay, chastising himself. "Especially after what happened to Helen." He turned to me, wanting reassurance. "But John's invitation sounded so sincere. I hated to turn it down."

"Just what was his invitation?"

"To come up for a few days and stay at his cabin. He'd be around," he said, "but never in the way. He had too many other irons in the fire."

"Did he say where he'd been for the past three years?"

"Traveling," he said. "From one end of the country to the other."

"Alone?" I asked.

That question haunted Devin LeMay, though he tried to hide it. "He said he'd been traveling alone. But I have my doubts."

"You think Helen was with him?"

He nodded. "At the first I thought so. I don't know where she is now."

"Which is one of the reasons you were so eager to see John Knight?"

"Yes," he admitted. "I thought if he knew where Helen was, he might tell me." Turning away, he picked up a pinecone and smelled it. "I still love her, you see, even after all of this time."

"And what was Diana to you?" I asked angrily. "A bargaining chip? You'd trade her to John Knight for information on Helen?"

That hit him hard. I guessed partly because there was some truth to it. "It wasn't like that," he said.

"Then how was it?"

**140**

He sighed, watching a pair of mallards land on Wild Horse Bay. "I wanted Diana along because I needed some moral support when I found John Knight. I had intended to confront him with the fact that he had stolen Helen from me. But I lacked the courage to face him alone. From our very first meeting I've lacked that kind of courage. Perhaps that's why whenever John and I were together, I always included Helen."

"Are you sure it wasn't the other way around?" I asked, as a second pair of mallards whisked in and landed on Wild Horse Bay. "Maybe Helen included herself at your expense because she wanted to be with him. As my Grandmother Ryland used to say, it takes two to tango."

"Helen was little more than a child," he said, bristling in her defense. "How was she to know the intentions of a John Knight?" He put his nose to the pinecone again, taking a deep breath. "I thought he was my friend. You can see how wrong I was."

"And when you got to Sand Lake?" I asked. "What happened then?" The air whistled with mallard wings as a flock flew in to join the others.

"John was already waiting for us here. It seemed we had hardly gotten to bed when I heard a knock at our cabin door. It was John. He said he was on his way into Orley for supplies and that he'd stop by for us on his way back. Which he did a few hours later."

"With or without supplies?" I asked.

"With," he answered. "He had his truck nearly loaded with them. I wondered how we could eat that much in a month, let alone a week." He brightened, struck with a sudden thought. "I guess that's why he wanted me to bring my boat. We would never have gotten all of that, us, and our luggage into that little boat of his." A second flock of mallards swooped in to join the rest. "Anyway, we loaded my boat, then tied his on behind mine, and pulled it. I could tell he was taken with Diana by the way he looked at her." He smiled warmly. "But then, nearly everybody is taken with Diana."

"Agreed," I said, not quite so warmly.

"It was a long hard trip," he continued. "It must have been afternoon by the time we portaged, switched boats, made a second trip back to the portage, and unloaded everything. Diana said she was exhausted, that she hadn't even worked that hard back at school, so she found a rock in the sun and went to lie on it. John meanwhile said to make ourselves at home, that he had a guiding job over on Lac LaCroix the next day, and would see us when he got back." Breaking the pinecone in two, he threw half of it in the direction of a red squirrel that had come halfway down a jack pine to bark at us. "I should have known by then something was wrong. When we got my boat unloaded, he made me hide it way back in the weeds where he said no one would find it. I asked him what were the chances of that happening anyway. He said you never know." One by one he began to strip the scales from the remaining half of the pine cone and flip these at the red squirrel. "After John left and while Diana slept, I began casting the shoreline and caught the largest pike of my life, one I couldn't wait to show Diana."

"The one whose head I saw on the skinning shed?" I interrupted.

A shadow crossed Devin LeMay's face and stayed there. "Yes. The same one," he said. "Diana fried part of it for our supper, and the rest we had to throw away because there wasn't any ice in the icebox." The shadow on his face deepened. "Then when I tried to start the generator later that evening, I couldn't find any gasoline, or kerosene for the lamps. Finally I had to light a fire in the fireplace just to see."

"What about all the supplies you brought with you?" I asked. "What did you do with those?" I didn't remember seeing any in John Knight's cabin.

"We didn't know what to do with them. John just dumped them in our laps and took off. Fortunately most of it was freezedried, canned, or powdered, so it wouldn't spoil."

"That seems more like survival supplies to me," I said.

"It did to me, too," he answered.

I studied Devin LeMay. He couldn't have been as naive as he seemed. Yet for the life of me I couldn't picture him as anything else. "Didn't you start to wonder at that point?" I asked.

"Of course I started to wonder. Diana and I both did, especially when we realized we were marooned there without a boat." He gave me a helpless look. "But what could we do? We couldn't very well swim for it."

"So what did you do?" I asked, noting that the sun was on its way down. We'd have to leave soon if we wanted to reach the Bumble Bee before dark.

"Made the most of it. Diana and I talked and drank wine until it was time to go to bed. Then I heard a noise outside and, thinking it might be a bear, went out to see. I don't know what happened next. Someone must have hit me from behind and locked me in that shed where you found the pike head."

"I also found a bucket of guts inside."

"For me," he said darkly. "In case I got hungry."

"And that was the last you saw of Diana?"

Devin LeMay began to slip away into his own thoughts. One of the reasons he looked so frail to me was that he was emaciated, his cheeks hollow, his bones

143

showing through his skin. But wrapped around the bones was a tough hard sinew that said he wasn't quite as frail as he appeared.

"That was the last I saw of her," he said quietly. "Hours later, I've no idea how many, I found that old broadax half buried in the dirt, and began to chop my way out with it." He looked at his hands, still blistered from his effort. "I don't know how long I was in there, whether one day or two, but it was afternoon before I saw daylight again, and evening before I could chop the hole large enough for me to crawl out." He bowed his head, staring wearily at the ground. "Diana was gone by then. So were all of the supplies."

"Do you have any idea where?"

He shook his head. "I've been all over this area looking. First in an old wooden canoe I found in the woods behind John's cabin. Then in my boat, when I finally found it again."

"Where did you find it?"

Keeping his eyes to the ground, he began stripping the pinecone again. "I don't remember. I'd know it again if I ever saw it. But I don't remember how I got there."

"Why haven't you gone for help?"

He stared blankly out across Wild Horse Bay. "I did go for help last night. At least I went to the Black Bear Lodge with the intention of asking for help. But everything was dark when I pulled in, and then someone came down to the pier to look into my boat."

"I was there," I said.

That surprised him. "I wish I had known. I thought it was somebody out to steal it, and that was the last thing I needed right then. So once I saw that the Black Bear Lodge was all closed up for the night, I left and went around to the other side of the lake where John had us leave the car. There I waited until daylight because I knew I couldn't go much farther without getting more gas."

"And today?" I asked, remembering that he'd left for Wild Horse Lake long before I did.

"I went searching again. There's so much lake here, so many bays and inlets, I always wonder what I might have overlooked." He stripped the last scale from the pinecone and threw the cone away. "On a hunch I swung into the Wild Horse River to see if John might have returned for something. You were on your way out while I was on my way in. Seeing you first, I pulled into the weeds and waited. From a distance, alone in a canoe, you looked like John to me." Turning his gaze on me, he said, "So I came after you."

"Had I been you, I would've done the same thing."

He didn't answer.

"No sign of him at all?" I asked.

"What's that?" He'd slipped a rung lower into his thoughts.

"In all of your searching you found no sign of John Knight or Diana at all?"

Again he didn't answer. I was afraid he wasn't going to.

"Devin?"

Slowly he reached into the pocket of his jeans and handed me the Indian bead necklace I'd given Diana the Christmas before. "I found this along a portage," he said.

"Where?" I asked, clutching the necklace so tightly I was afraid I'd break it.

"The same place where I found my boat."

"But you can't remember where that is?" I could hardly stand to look at him.

"No," he answered. "I remember the portage led

**145**

into a large lake on the other side . . . but I couldn't carry the canoe across . . . so I got into my boat and tried to go around . . ." He began to chop his words. "Then I lost my way."

I rose to my feet. A few seconds later Devin LeMay rose to his and meekly followed me down to the lake.

# 11

*I* filled the motor with the last of the gas and drove the canoe south toward the Bumble Bee Resort. Fresh from the north, the wind helped us along, making the gas go farther than it should have. Still I had to paddle the last mile, and it was nearly dark when we glided into shore.

The old man hobbled down to the water's edge to help me land. Then he noticed Devin LeMay hunched in the bow of the canoe. He spoke in greeting. Devin didn't answer. He'd slipped into a silence that had grown deeper as the miles passed.

"What's wrong with him?" the old man asked.

"Battle fatigue," I said in Devin's defense.

"He seems to have a bad case of it."

Devin, if he overheard our conversation, chose to ignore it. "Yes, he does have a bad case of it," I agreed. "Any chance you can put us up for the night?"

**147**

The old man nodded toward the pines. "I've got a whole row of empty cabins. Take your pick."

"Number one," Devin mumbled. "I want cabin number one."

The old man must have seen my face. "Is that okay with you, son?" he asked.

"Yeah, it'll do." But I didn't convince either one of us.

Leaning on his cane, the old man bent over to examine his canoe. "Better shape than I thought it'd be," he said.

I handed him his tattered map. "That makes two of us."

Together the old man and I helped Devin to cabin number one, where we eased him down on a bed. On the way to get Jessie and my suitcase I told the old man what had happened and where the remains of Devin's boat could be found. Silent for a moment, he said, "I wonder what got into that boy. He could've gotten the both of you killed."

"I think John Knight got into him," I said. "Whether Devin knows it or not, it's been building for at least three years now."

"It doesn't look like it's getting any better," he observed. "I've never seen a man lower in my life than that boy is."

I put my arm around him as we walked up the hill to his store. "No. It doesn't look like it to me either."

Back at cabin number one Devin hadn't moved from his bed. I opened my suitcase and took out a bar of Ivory soap and a change of clothes. "Anything in here you'd like?" I asked him.

He lay on his back, staring at the ceiling. "No thanks."

"Anything I can get you before I take a bath?"

148

"No, thanks."

The first rush of cold lake water took my breath away, but after that it felt good. Soaping myself all over, I climbed up on the pier and dived in, then puttered around in the water, like a kid playing hooky from school. The moon came over the pines and dappled the lake. A loon chuckled to himself over a private joke. I smelled the pines, the water, and the Ivory soap, and felt cleaner than I had for a long, long time.

The feeling lasted all the way to cabin number one. But when I opened the door and turned on the light, I wanted to go no farther. It took all of my will to drive me over the threshold and inside to Devin LeMay.

"The water's fine," I said, closing the door behind me. "You sure you don't want to try it?"

"No, thanks," he said. "Maybe in the morning."

"Suit yourself." I put on my clean clothes. They felt good.

"Where are you going?" he asked, showing interest for the first time since we landed.

"I'm not sure yet. I just want to go out for a while."

"I understand." He couldn't hide his disappointment.

"You can come along if you like." I tried to sound sincere.

"No. I'd rather stay here."

"You're sure?"

"Yes. I'll be fine by myself."

"I won't be gone long," I said. "I'll just take a walk or something and come right back."

He rolled over, hiding his face from me. "I'll be fine, really. Go ahead."

"Is there anything I can bring you to eat?" I asked.

"No. I'm not hungry."

"How about to drink?"

He rolled my way, thought about it a moment, then said, "A root beer, please."

"I'll see what I can do."

The old man lived in two rooms at the back of his store. He had an early photograph of his wife and their three sons in a birch frame upon his desk, a small birch bed nestled against one wall of his bedroom, and a small pine table for two in the kitchen, where he sat eating his supper. He'd fried himself a salmon patty, along with a skillet of potatoes and onions. To me, who had last eaten a peanut butter and jelly sandwich on my way to Wild Horse Lake, it looked and smelled like a feast.

"Pull up a chair," he said. "There's enough for both of us. If not, I'll make more."

I was tempted, but I knew what he'd made wouldn't feed both of us, and I didn't want him waiting on me. "Thanks," I said. "But I really came after a root beer for Devin. He doesn't want anything to eat, but he did say he'd drink a root beer."

"I'm not surprised," he said, wiping some grease from his chin. "That's all that boy drank when he was up here with his grandmother. I had to lay in an extra case just for him."

"Any chance there's still some around?"

"I'll have to see," he said, in no hurry to move. "So you might as well join me before it gets cold."

"I'd like to," I said. "But I'm a little restless tonight. It's hard for me to stay in one place for long."

"I know the feeling," he said. "I get the same way when the wind comes up fresh and the pines are smelling sweet. Especially after a rain." He smiled at me. "It's the north, got into your blood."

"Something anyway," I agreed.

"So where are you headed to?" he asked.

"I'm not sure yet. Who around here can best tell me where John Knight might have taken Diana?"

He thought a moment, then said, "That'd probably be Patsy Bircher."

"I don't know how far I'd get," I said. "I don't think I'm Patsy Bircher's favorite person."

He smiled in understanding. "She give you the cold shoulder?"

"That's probably an understatement."

"Don't feel like the odd man out. She treats just about everybody that way." He ate a bite of salmon. "You can't blame her much, though. For one thing she's running her own business, and that's never easy, especially up here. For another, she's not had much luck where men are concerned. Her first husband about drank the business under before he fell out of a boat and drowned. Her second husband nearly stole her blind before he took off. Then long ago, before any of the others, the boy she loved fell through the ice while running his trap line, and drowned." He blinked a couple times, then looked down at his plate and loaded his fork with potatoes and onions. "That's the son I told you about, the one I lost to the lake."

"Then along came John Knight," I said.

He nodded, but didn't look up. "Then along came John Knight."

I drove to the Black Bear Lodge. Patsy Bircher stood behind the bar. One glance said she already knew what I planned to ask her. Her C.B. buzzed in the background as someone talked about finding the wreckage of Devin LeMay's boat.

"What do you know about that?" she demanded.

"It's not John Knight's, if that's what you're worried about."

"You're sure?" she asked, relieved.

"Yes. I was there."

Someone at the other end of the bar raised an empty glass. As she took off in that direction, I noticed the man in the mirror facing me. He didn't look like a man who that very day had run from his own shadow. With his plaid wool shirt, rumpled hair, and beard he almost seemed at home there in the north. And yet his eyes gave him away. They didn't have the clear clean certainty of the North. There was too much irony in them, too many unanswered questions for single-minded purpose. He wouldn't last six months up there before he started talking to the moose and otters, taking his pen and notebook in hand and asking them what they thought about it all.

Reaching into my wallet, I took out Diana's photograph to make sure it had survived the day. Taken in one of our lighter moments at an antique car rally, it captured her standing next to her yellow Bentley with her head thrown back, just enough leg showing, and a hint of a smile. I smiled back at her. How long ago had that been?

"Who's that?" Patsy Bircher asked.

"A friend."

"Let me see it."

I handed Diana's photograph to her. Patsy Bircher had rough thick hands and wrists nearly the size of mine, but she handled the photograph with infinite care. "I like her," she said, handing Diana's photograph back to me. "But I don't think she's your type."

I put Diana's photograph back into my wallet. "Why do you say that?" I asked.

"Because she doesn't know who she is. You do."

I rose to Diana's defense. "In time she'll learn."

"None of us have that much time to waste."

"You might be right," I agreed.

"I know I am," she answered, wiping the bar clean in front of me. "Now, what'll you have?"

I wanted answers, but they could wait. "A shot of your best rye."

"My very best?"

"If I can afford it."

"I think you can."

She brought it to me. I sipped it, savoring the taste, feeling it warm me all the way down. When I could see bottom, I ordered another. Patsy Bircher joined me. It was a slow Sunday night at the Black Bear Lodge.

"I suppose the kitchen's closed," I said.

"It is. But what would you like?"

"The thickest steak you have."

"Medium-rare?"

"Yes. Medium-rare."

Several minutes later she brought me a porterhouse steak that hung over both sides of the platter. Tender, cooked to perfection, it reminded me of a steak I once had somewhere in Arizona. Served by a beautiful Apache who, like Patsy Bircher, ran the whole show herself, it would forever remain the standard by which I judged the steaks of the world.

"Whose boat was it there on the reef?" she asked, pouring herself a second glass of rye. The last person in the coffee shop besides us had just left.

I told her whose boat it was and how it got there. Patsy Bircher sat staring at herself in the bar mirror. I sat staring at my steak, wondering if I dared finish it. "Do you have any idea where John Knight might be?" I asked.

She looked at me and shrugged. Tears came into her eyes. "No," she said quietly.

"Are you still in love with him?"

"I don't know. Why does that matter?"

**153**

"I was just curious. You seem to know what he is, that you have known all along. So I wondered how you could still love him."

She rose and returned a moment later with the drawing I'd admired earlier that day, which seemed, by Garth time, about a hundred years ago. It was the drawing of the pine, star, and grouse that captured the lonely essence of the north.

"You offered to buy it this morning," she said. "Are you still interested?"

I took the drawing in hand. Each time I looked at it I saw something more. "Would you sell it to me?"

She shook her head no. "I'd give up my life first."

Studying the drawing more closely, I searched for flaws and found none. "Are you telling me that John Knight did this?"

"No. A friend of mine did this when we were eighteen, a few days before he fell through the ice and drowned. His name was also John, John Swanson, and he was like the north itself, as headstrong and unforgiving . . . But there was something else about him . . ." Her eyes shone as she spoke. "Something that was pure and beautiful; something that took my breath away when I first glimpsed it . . . and every time after that." She picked up the drawing, caressing it. "When you've lost a John Swanson, what can a John Knight ever really do to hurt you?" After a moment, Patsy Bircher noticed I wasn't saying anything. "What's wrong?" she asked.

I shook my head. "Nothing."

A man came into the room and started to take a seat at the bar. "I'm sorry," Patsy Bircher said. "We're closed."

He glanced at me. "You don't look closed."

154

Escorting him to the door, she said, "I know. It's a private party."

He shrugged and walked out. She locked the door behind him.

"Is that good for business?" I asked.

"Probably not. But tonight I don't care."

"You're the boss," I reminded her.

She glanced around the room at all the things unfinished and undone. "How could I ever forget."

I stretched and yawned. The day had begun to take its toll on me. All the bumps and bruises I'd ignored until then began to make themselves felt.

"You should go to bed," she said.

"That's what I keep telling myself." Though I hated the thought of spending the night in cabin number one with Devin LeMay.

"Mine's available," she said.

I smiled at her, hoping she'd understand. "Thanks. But I can't."

"For whose sake, yours or hers?"

"Does it matter?"

"Walk me to my door, then?" she asked.

"Sure."

She let me out the door, locking it behind her. Clear, crisp, and freshly washed, the northern sky held too many stars even to try to count. We walked through the woods along a path to her cabin. On a thousand other nights in my life, I would have followed her inside.

"You won't find him," she said, opening the door. "You won't find John Knight. Not alive anyway."

She was the second person to tell me that. John Knight's mother was the first. "What do you know that I don't?" I asked.

"I know John," she answered. "He'll never let himself be locked up. He'd die first."

"He's told you that?"

"In a moment of weakness," she replied.

"Then what are Diana's chances of coming out of this alive?" I asked.

"Not good," she said. "If you call out the authorities on him."

"I won't, then."

"That's wise."

Before she could close the door, I asked a second time. "Are you sure you don't have some idea of where he might have taken her? Devin LeMay mentioned a portage that led from Sand Lake into another large lake."

"That could be one of many," she answered. "Do you know how much water there is in Sand Lake alone? Multiply that by ten thousand, and that's how much water there is up here."

"Are you saying to give it up as a lost cause?"

"No," she said softly. "Because you won't."

"What are you saying, then?"

She gave me the best advice anyone had for a long time. "Search wherever you like for as long as you like, and when you've given up hope, look in your heart. That's where you'll find her."

"If she can be found," I said, wanting reassurance.

But Patsy Bircher was fresh out of answers. "I would say that's up to you."

# 12

The old man sat on the porch of the store when I returned to the Bumble Bee. Together we watched the northern lights dazzle the stars. "I took the boy his root beer," the old man said. "But I couldn't get him to eat anything."

"How's he doing?" I asked.

"His spirits seem to be on the rebound, but he looks thin enough to crawl through a keyhole. When was the last time he ate anything?"

"I don't know. I'm not sure he even knows."

"It sounds like Winter Knight led him a merry chase."

"As he has all of us," I said.

We sat for a while, watching the sky. The northern lights were about played out, their afterglow a faint reminder of their earlier brilliance. I looked at the old man. His eyes were lit by the same soft afterglow, his fire steeped for the night.

"A penny for your thoughts," I said.

He continued to watch the sky. "I'd rather have yours."

"I'm not sure mine are worth much," I answered.

He turned to me, a smile playing at the corners of his mouth. "Not even a penny?" he asked.

Watching a shooting star streak the sky overhead, I wondered how many millions of years had just exploded before my eyes. "Something happened to me on the way up to John Knight's cabin," I said. "I felt afraid, a real fear of death, for the first time in my life." Another star burned itself out. "I felt it once before, back home when I fell through the ice on Willoby's Slough, but that was a different kind of fear, one I could see, know, and understand. But today it seemed to come from outside of me and force its way into my soul. I couldn't control it, only run from it."

"And that bothers you?" he asked.

"It bothers the hell out of me, if you want the truth."

He stared out across Sand Lake, dark and murmuring and, in its depths, still rippling from the storm. "Maybe you grew a couple inches today," he said. "Have you ever thought of that?"

"In what way?" I asked.

"Wisdom, horsesense, understanding, whatever it is you want to call it. We can go our whole lives on the same straight track and think that's all there is to it. And we're smart, I guess, in our own way, if we're learning as we go. But it seems to me the wise man changes directions more often than most. Still keeping to the same track, wherever his truth leads him, and not running in circles like some people do, but willing to

158

make those hard turns whenever life asks it of him, and not dragging one foot as he does." He smiled at me. "For a young man you seem to have a pretty good handle on things. So don't be too hard on yourself. You looked fear in the eye today, and he stared you down. But then again maybe he should have."

"Maybe," I said. "But that doesn't make me feel any better about myself."

He turned away from me to gaze once more at the sky. "It's not supposed to make you feel any better. Only to point out something you might have missed."

"Do you believe I did the right thing?" I asked.

"By turning tail and running?"

"Yes."

His eyes sharpened as he looked my way. "You're alive, aren't you?"

"But I abandoned my search for Diana, the one I came up here to find. And in the end I ran into danger, not away from it. I nearly got run over by a boat because I turned tail."

He shrugged, using his cane to draw a bead on the North Star. "You can't tell. You just never can tell."

We sat for a few more minutes until I got chilled. "Well," I said. "I'd better call it a day."

"Here," he said, handing me a key. "It's to cabin number two. I've already moved your suitcase and dusted things off in there."

"How did you know?" I asked.

"Had my wife spent the night with another man someplace, I might have a hard time sleeping there, too." He buttoned his black wool sweater, and it appeared he'd be staying for a while longer. "The motor's all gassed up and ready to go when you are," he said. "You'll find another map of Sand Lake there on the table in your cabin."

"Thanks doesn't even come close," I said.

For the first time he was at a momentary loss for words. "Close or not, it'll have to do."

I liked the feel of cabin number two. Larger than cabin number one, but not too large to be cozy, it had the clean bold scent of the north. I lit a gas lamp and undressed. Soft and bright, the whispery light sang to me its lullaby.

But I couldn't sleep. I dressed and went for a walk. Lightly tossing the aspens, the west wind blew at my back as I walked along the path toward the dump. Then, as the hair on my nape rose in warning, I realized something was stalking me.

A bear, I thought at first. I could smell him, feel his nearness press down on me, anchoring my feet to the ground. Afraid to move, afraid even to take a deep breath, I stood, feeling my legs go wooden and sink into the path like cedar posts. An owl passed overhead. Its shadow swam specterlike over the forest floor, the deep *hoot, hoot* of its hunting call sudden and fierce.

I found a rock underfoot and nudged it loose. Kneeling, I tossed it sidearm into the brush. The woods erupted as something large and powerful went crashing through the brush ahead of me. I waited several heartbeats, long enough for a single small cloud to find the moon, before walking on. Still I felt something stalking me.

At the edge of the dump I found Devin LeMay's car and John Knight's truck where we'd found them earlier that morning. A couple of stray dogs prowled the dump. The dogs took little notice of me as they fed on the remains of a deer carcass that someone had dumped there. At least I assumed it was a deer. All I could see were entrails and four hooved legs.

I found Devin LeMay's boat trailer hidden in the

weeds where he said he'd left it. Ensnarled in woody tendrils that bound it tighter the harder I pulled, it resisted all my efforts to move it. Then with a lunge I tore it free. Satisfied that I'd accomplished at least one thing on a day of failures, I left the trailer at the edge of the weeds a few feet from where I'd found it.

All the way back to cabin number two I felt that same something following me. Twice I stopped suddenly in the path and turned around, but saw nothing there. Once inside the cabin, I locked the door, turned off the gaslight, and waited at the window, but nothing appeared. Had I not felt a presence so strongly, I would have thought my mind was playing tricks on me.

Closing the curtains, I relit the gas lamp and sat at the table studying the map the old man left for me. Patsy Bircher was right. There was a lot of water up there. Its expanse seemed almost infinite.

I rose before dawn and took a moment to stretch the kinks out before moving any farther. My knees hurt from where I'd banged them on the reef. My shin had an ugly bruise on it from my fall in the rock gorge. My whole body ached from the strain of the previous day, in muscles I didn't even know I had. But at that I felt lucky. Had I been a few seconds later in clearing the Wild Horse River, or had Devin LeMay been a few seconds earlier . . . I left it there. Like the old man said, I was alive, wasn't I? No need to dwell on might-have-beens.

The old man knocked at the door. "Here's a lunch I packed for you," he said. "There's a little something to get your day started in there, too."

"Thanks," I said.

"It'll be on your bill," he replied with a twinkle in his eye.

A few minutes later I hurried down to the lake to

161

make sure I left before Devin LeMay awakened. On that particular day I didn't want anyone's company in my search for Diana. I wanted my thoughts, and the azure waters of Sand Lake, to myself.

My spirits fell. Not even the first burst of sunlight across Sand Lake could raise them up again. Dressed in his jeans, deck shoes, and green polo shirt, Devin LeMay sat hunched in the bow of the old man's boat waiting for me.

"Good morning!" he said cheerily. "I'd about given up on you."

"Good morning," I answered. "Are you sure you're up to this?"

"Why wouldn't I be?" he replied. Then he asked, "What's in the sack?"

"Breakfast and lunch. There's coffee and sweet rolls if you'd like." My coffee, my sweet rolls. Part of me said that's okay, Garth, because he needs it more than you do. The other part, the one that got out of sorts whenever I didn't eat, wanted to drop him on the nearest rock.

"Thanks," he said, taking the sack from me. "I don't mind if I do."

We pushed off and headed north, with me in the stern running the motor and he in the bow feeding his face. He'd finished the coffee and both sweet rolls before we were out of sight of the Bumble Bee, then he ate one of the sandwiches that were to be my lunch. He then rolled the sack up and set it in the bottom of the canoe at his feet.

We put the narrows behind us and continued on north. Bathed in the first light of day, the rocks along the west shoreline yawned and glistened, while those on the east shoreline, still in shadows, slept the morning away. Gulls rose from their rock island roosts and

162

came out shrieking to greet us, then turned away when they saw we weren't fishermen. The few boats we met on their way south down the lake did little to disturb the tranquillity. Like us, they seemed to belong there.

I had a plan. We'd start at the north edge of Wild Horse Bay and work our way along the shoreline until we came to the first inlet that promised a lake beyond. After exploring that inlet, depending on whether we found anything or not, we'd continue on north around the lake until we finally ran out of shoreline. If we were lucky, we might find something that day. If my luck ran as it usually did, I could count on spending Christmas there.

"What are you doing?" Devin asked when we pulled into the first inlet.

"Looking for the portage where you found Diana's necklace."

"This isn't it," he insisted.

"Then tell me where it is."

"I already told you, I don't know." Angry that I'd asked him again, he turned away to stare out the bow of the boat. "I don't like to be reminded of that," he said. "If you want the truth of the matter."

"But if you don't know where it is, how am I supposed to know that this isn't it?"

"You'll just have to take my word for it."

"Fair enough," I said, conceding to him more power than I wanted to. Devin was then in charge of the search instead of me.

We went from bay to bay, inlet to inlet, river to river, but nothing looked familiar to him. Toward afternoon I asked for the sack to see if there was anything left to eat in it, but when he threw it to me, it sailed over my head and landed in Sand Lake. By the time I retrieved it, I had a soggy egg salad sandwich and a watery dill pickle. I ate them anyway.

Rounding what seemed like our hundredth bend, we came to an inlet that looked like all the others to me. But Devin, who had faithfully maintained his vigil throughout the day, suddenly shouted, "This is it! I'm sure of it!"

"How can you tell?"

"It just feels right to me."

We entered a small stagnant river, which, if it flowed at all, did so without moving a reed. Even the yellow aspen leaves floating upon it lay dead in the water, stirred only by an occasional puff of wind. "I don't think this is it," I said.

Without a channel to follow through the weeds, I had to raise the motor and paddle the canoe. It was hard going with the two of us in there and only one paddling. Neither could Devin sit still. In his growing excitement he kept leaning from side to side, threatening to tip us over.

"Sure this is it," he insisted. "I know I've been here before!"

"Then what should we look for?" I asked.

"A bluff," he said. "There'll be a bluff ahead and a rapids through it. You can portage around the rapids or climb the bluff, whichever you choose, but they both lead to a huge lake on the other side."

He seemed so certain and so happy to have found it that I couldn't tell him that neither bluff nor rapids lay ahead. The map didn't show it if they did. And as the river was too still and sullen to contain a rapids, the lay of the land itself was too low and marshy to grow a bluff. Devin LeMay saw with his heart instead of his eyes.

"How much farther?" I asked. The weeds began to

close in on us, wrap themselves around my paddle and tug at the canoe.

"Not much," he said. "It'll open up again in a minute, you'll see." But the certainty had left his voice.

We came to a cluster of weeds too dense to paddle through. Surrounding us, the land looked spongy and boglike, and not the kind of terrain I'd want to try to walk. As far as I was concerned, it was the end of the line.

"We can't go any farther," I said.

"What do you mean we can't go any farther?" he shouted. "The rapids are just ahead!"

"Devin, you want to believe that. For both our sakes I'd like to believe that. But they're not."

"They are!" he cried. "I'm telling you, they are!"

"Then where is the path you made through the weeds to get here? And where is the boat you left behind?"

He frantically searched the weeds for a path through them. Then in a leap that also sent me into the river to save the canoe and motor, he plunged into the water and began thrashing toward what he thought was shore.

I couldn't stop him. I was too busy trying to retrieve the canoe, which had shot out from under us and slid several yards away. A weed brushed my leg. Another weed caressed my shoulder before wrapping itself around my neck, dragging me under. Fighting panic and my innate fear of depths and all other closed-in places, I felt the pressure rise in my brain. I kicked out, caught another weed, and was dragged even lower. Air! My lungs screamed at me. Air! Tearing myself free from the weeds, I thrust upward and began to claw my way to the surface. Gone were all thoughts of retrieving the canoe. I only wanted not to drown.

I surfaced with a gasp, took one sweet gulp of air, and hung there gatorlike, trying to decide what to do next. The canoe had drifted deeper into the weeds. A huge anvil cloud had darkened the sky, and a mist began to fall. The mist fattened to drizzle, drizzle to rain. Lowering all the while, the sky slowly sank into the trees.

I needed to move. Though I was out of wind, the water was still September-cold, its numbing pressure ever present. My legs began to cramp, and my shoulders ached. Rain mixed with salt and ran into my eyes. An hour before, under a warm sun and a blue sky, finding Diana had been my only problem. How quickly things changed in the north.

What seemed like hours later, after a treacherous swim through the weeds that left me exhausted, I found a stump, crawled back into the canoe, and sat there bent and shivering, searching for Devin LeMay. At first I saw only reeds and wild rice and, out where Sand Lake joined the river, a sheet of pitted slate, the gray monotony of rain upon the water. Then I saw that he, too, had found a stump, and sat there posed and still, like a wooden Indian. Neither did he greet me when I approached him in the canoe. Instead he sank lower into his gloom until his face matched the sky.

"Devin, it's time for one of us to go home," I said. When he didn't answer, I added, "All we're doing is getting in each other's way. For Diana's sake we need to do better than that."

He looked at me—his eyes red and angry—as though he had been betrayed. "Home? Where do you mean, home?"

"Home to Madison. Or to Oakalla, whatever the case may be."

"I haven't found her," he said. "How can you ask me to go home?"

"How much farther can you go?" I asked.

He turned away to gaze at something only he could see. "No farther," he said wearily.

"Then you've done all you can."

"Will you stay and look for her?" he said, turning back to me. "And not give up until you find her?"

"Yes. I'll stay," I said.

"For how long?"

"As long as it takes to find her." I didn't see the need to repeat myself, but if that's what it took to get rid of him, I would have repeated it again and again.

That seemed to satisfy him. "I have your word?"

"You have my word."

Using the paddle as a brake, I steadied the canoe as he crawled gingerly back into it. He shivered from the wet and cold, but I had no dry clothes to offer him.

We soon left the river and headed out across the main body of Sand Lake. The rain continued to fall, the sky stayed low, and my spirits continued to sink along with those of Devin LeMay. By the time we reached the Bumble Bee, wet, hungry, and nearly numb with cold, neither one of us felt like talking.

But then I saw a familiar figure standing on the dock in the rain, looking as forlorn as I felt. In all of my life, I had never been happier to see anyone.

# 13

Sheriff Rupert Roberts held out his hand, large and calloused like his life, and pulled us in to shore. His face, perpetually somber, broke into a smile that threatened to crack wide open. Then we stood with nothing to say, until he reached for his tobacco pouch and offered it to me. I shook my head and smiled. We were back on familiar ground.

"There were times when I wasn't sure I'd be here either," I said. "But here I am."

"You could be happier about it," he said.

"I'll tell you about it later."

Despite our protests, Devin LeMay wouldn't stay another night and start for Madison in the morning. As soon as the canoe hit shore, he jumped out and strode up the path toward cabin number one. Once there, he took only a moment to survey it before moving on. The look on his face said that this would be his last trip to Sand Lake.

"What do you want me to do with your clothes?" I asked, as he started up the path to the dump.

"What clothes?"

"The ones you left in John Knight's cabin."

"Do whatever you like with them. I don't ever want to see them again."

"I'll call you as soon as I learn anything," I promised.

"Only if it's good news." He turned and started walking.

"Have a safe trip home," I said.

If he heard, he didn't answer.

He left, and as I watched him growing gradually smaller until the woods swallowed him altogether, I felt a great surge of relief, as though someone had just removed a millstone from around my neck. Twice in two days he had put us both in the water and nearly gotten us killed. In the north, the third time might prove a charm.

Together Rupert and I built a roaring fire in cabin number two, then I took off my wet clothes and hung them up to dry. But even that didn't warm me. Not completely. Inside, right next to my heart, I still felt cold.

The old man told us that cabin number two was the oldest of the nine rental cabins. He and his wife had bought the cabin from a trapper in the 1940s, intending to rent it out, but had decided instead to live there while building the other cabins. Over the years they had added an oil stove, a gas refrigerator, and a gas cook stove, wider windows so his wife could see the lake better, and a second bedroom and bunk beds as their boys got older. In their later years they'd finally added electricity and running water. And yet the old man, like me, still preferred the gaslights to sit and think by.

Without phone, stereo, or television, cabin number two was the perfect place for cards, books, or conversation, or if you came up with someone you loved, the perfect place to curl up together and forget the world for a while. I wished Diana and I could have had a week there. It would have been the perfect place to say good-bye.

I poked the fire and added another log. No matter how close I sat to the hearth or how high the flames rose, I couldn't shake the chill, or the gloom that had settled into me.

"Is something eating at you, Garth?" Rupert said.

Staring into the fire, I wanted to explain, but wasn't sure I could. "It's a perfect place for a honeymoon, isn't it?" I said.

"It's a perfect place for anything, it seems to me," he said. "What's your point?"

"Diana could have come up here with me. Instead she came up with Devin LeMay." I continued to stare into the fire. "I guess that's my point."

"You having second thoughts about her?" he asked.

"Second, third, and fourth," I said. "But that still doesn't change how I feel about her."

"Maybe nothing ever will," he offered. "Maybe those feelings will stay in you right on up until the day you die. But in the meantime someone else might come along who wants a whole lot more of you than she does. So while you might still have the same feelings for her, they won't count for as much as they once did."

"Is that what happened to you?" I asked.

"In a manner of speaking."

"Whom did you love before Elvira came along?"

170

"Nobody that you know, Garth."

Someone knocked at the door. As Rupert rose to answer it, the old man entered carrying a bottle of bourbon and a bag of popcorn. "Open a window," he said, taking off his flannel shirt. "It's hot enough to roast a turkey in here."

Early the next morning Rupert and I left in the old man's canoe to set up a base camp at the north end of Sand Lake. A mist hung gauzelike over the water. The sun burned red, then orange, then white, as the air warmed and the mist thinned. Late-rising and slow to take shape, it was a morning that let us set our own pace.

"Who's minding the store back home?" I asked Rupert as we passed through the narrows and broke into the sunlight on the other side.

"Clarkie is," he said with great restraint.

"And how's Ruth?" I asked.

"Worried about you. But other than that she's still the same."

"Is she the one who sent you up here?"

"It was sort of a mutual agreement," he answered. "We both thought you could use some help."

Shielding my eyes from the sun, I steered clear of a large rock. "And you were right," I said.

For our base camp we chose an island north of Wild Horse Bay near the east shore of Sand Lake. With pines to the north and west and a bluff to the south to break the wind, the island had a small sand beach protected on all sides but the east, and a spongy bed of moss-covered granite on the leeward side where we decided to pitch our tent.

We'd just driven our last stake when the sun went under and the first drops of rain began to fall. For the next two days we had the same mixed bag of rain, sun, clouds, and blue. We'd gear ourselves up for rain, have the sun come out a few minutes later, start to sweat, take off our rain suits, and put them on within the hour after another rain blew in. The uncertainty of the weather and the enormity of our search put both of us on edge and left little room for conversation.

Then Patsy Bircher flew in to tell us that in her flights over Sand Lake and the lakes beyond she hadn't sighted anyone who resembled either John Knight or Diana. Neither had any of the other pilots she'd talked to. Rupert and I shared a grim look of acknowledgment. Of all the campers, canoers, and fishermen we'd asked, none had seen John Knight either.

Late Wednesday evening the sky cleared and promised fair weather at least until morning. Rupert and I built a campfire out of driftwood, then sat close as we cooked a can of beef stew. Unusually silent all day, Rupert had kept his thoughts to himself and his eyes on the shoreline, speaking only when spoken to. I thought I knew what was bothering him, but was afraid to ask for fear he'd tell me. At nightfall, while we watched Mars brighten the southern sky, the moment finally came for him to speak his mind.

"Garth," he said. "I think it's time we went home, and turned this over to somebody up here."

"You go ahead," I answered, picking up a stick and poking it into the fire. "I'm not quite ready yet."

"No," he said. "I mean it's time for both of us to go. You've been up here long enough."

"Less than a week," I pointed out, using the glowing end of the stick to draw orange circles in the air.

"Longer," he said. "When you count the days from when you first started to let yourself go, it's more like three weeks."

"I haven't let myself go," I insisted.

"You haven't put much time in taking care of yourself either."

"That doesn't matter to me," I said. "Nothing does except finding Diana."

He didn't answer.

"Or don't you think she's worth it?" I asked.

He pinched off a chew and studied it a moment before putting it into his mouth. Meanwhile my stick had lost its glow. I threw it into the fire.

"She's not worth your life," he answered. "Which is what you're trying to give her."

"Bullshit," I said.

I didn't ruffle a feather. "What do you mean bullshit?" he asked, staring into the fire.

"Put yourself in my shoes," I said. "Are you saying that if Elvira were in John Knight's hands instead of Diana, you wouldn't overturn every rock, search every lake and island, every inch of shoreline until you found her, no matter how long it took? I know you better than that, Rupert."

He spat into the fire, which hissed back at him. "Elvira is my wife, and has been for forty-two years."

"The principle's the same," I argued.

"No, it's not the same. You don't have forty-two years invested in her. Forty-two years of making a home and a living, and raising three children, and stretching a dollar so thin you could see through it. You haven't been through all the pains and the sorrows and the joys . . ." He stopped to watch a shooting star. "All the temptations and the reunions, and the swallowing of your pride and saying I'm sorry, even when you know you aren't." He again spat into the fire. "Your life won't end with Diana, whether you find her or not. But if something were to happen to Elvira, I don't know

173

what I'd do. Go on, I guess, because I don't know any better. But I'd be hard-pressed to find any point in it."

"I feel the same way about Diana," I said.

"Do you, Garth?" he challenged me. "Then why aren't you married to her? And why did she come up here with Devin LeMay instead of you?"

Picking up a pinecone, I threw it into the fire and watched it burn. "You know why. She's not ready for that kind of commitment."

"She's nearly forty years old, Garth. When will she be ready?"

I shook my head. "I don't know."

"Maybe she'll never be ready. Have you ever thought of that? Maybe she's one of those people who do better by themselves because they're the only person they have to answer to."

I reached for another pinecone, but didn't throw it into the fire. "She was married to Fran for over fifteen years. How do you explain that?"

"That's easy enough," he said. "You ask a lot more out of her than Fran Baldwin ever did. With him all she had to do was to play the role she chose for herself. With you she'd have to dig a lot deeper, and maybe come up empty."

"I don't understand."

He turned to me, his eyes large and wise. "That's because you don't want to. You want to believe that she loves you the same as you love her. But she doesn't, Garth. For all of her good looks, talent, and intelligence, she doesn't have it in her."

"She has it in her," I insisted. "She just hasn't found it yet."

He turned back to gaze into the fire. "It seems to me that amounts to the same thing."

I tossed the pinecone off into the night, and I never

heard it land. "Even if that's true, and I'm not saying I agree it is, I just can't leave her here and go home."

"Why?"

I shrugged. I wished I had the pinecone back. "It's hard to explain. I don't even know what it is that drives me, but something does, and it has its own mind. It's not just pride, or stubbornness, or a search for truth, or anything as simple as that. I can't quit because it's in my blood not to quit, because the times I have quit on something that really mattered to me, I've regretted it ever since."

"You quit on your marriage," he pointed out. "How is this different?"

"I only quit on my marriage after I knew it was hopeless. Not before."

He nodded ever so slightly, as if he understood.

"Then you'll stay and help me?"

"I'll stay," he promised. "For at least another day."

The brilliance of the dawn gave every indication that fair skies would last throughout the day. Helped along by the hint of a south wind that barely wrinkled the surface of Sand Lake, we motored far to the west and entered a large bay that neither one of us remembered seeing before. Two great boulders guarded the mouth of the bay. To enter we had to pass directly between them. In the bay itself boulders were strewn about like a giant's blocks, and with no apparent channel to follow, we had to carefully pick and choose our route carefully, or risk losing our prop to the outcroppings below.

With both hands cupped over his eyes, Rupert leaned over the bow of the canoe to guide me. I followed his lead, expecting to hear the prop strike a rock at any moment. When we reached the point where we couldn't stand the tension anymore, we stopped to rest our nerves.

"How much farther, do you think," I asked, "before we get out of the rocks?"

"A couple hundred yards at the most."

"What then?"

He spat into the water. "I don't know. I was hoping you could tell me."

We continued to weave our way through the rocks until we came to an inner bay that shone sapphire-blue in the sun. High bluffs surrounded it, held immense pines and grandeur. I looked at Rupert. Rupert looked at me. We both felt the same awe.

As though cleaving the face of a great blue jewel, we cut a diagonal across the bay, our divided wake reaching both shores at the same time. Struck by the solitude that we had destroyed by the harsh thrash of our wake against the bluffs, I felt we'd cut the heart of the north itself, and what we saw pouring into the bay was not a river but a vein of pure blue blood rushing in from the forest to repair the damage we'd done. Then I saw a wooden canoe bobbing and whirling in the white eddies at the river's mouth—possibly John Knight's canoe by the looks of it.

"This might be it!" I said to Rupert. "This looks like the place Devin LeMay told me about, where he found Diana's necklace."

"You're sure?" He wasn't convinced.

We pulled alongside the canoe. Flecked and weathered, it had moss growing along the gunnels. "If I wasn't before, I am now."

Too impatient to take the long portage through the woods, I stripped to my jeans and T-shirt and pulled off my shoes and socks before starting up the bluff. I felt the lightest I had in years, and more surefooted than even as a boy. "I'm coming, Diana!" I shouted. "It won't be long now."

But as the sun went under a cloud, a sharp gust of wind nudged me dangerously close to the edge of the bluff, and I had to drop to my knees to keep from going over. Glancing at the sky, I saw a tower of clouds building toward the sun. Glancing over my shoulder, I saw just where I was—on the highest, steepest face of the bluff.

The sun peeked out again, igniting the bluff, which glared like a hot white eye, daring me to scale it. I searched for another way up, but was blocked on either side by a smooth stretch of granite too sheer to traverse. Taking a deep breath to calm myself, I knew I didn't dare look down to Rupert below, or I would see all the reasons not to go on.

I waited for the exact moment when my heart said *Go!*, leapt up, slipped, tried to shoot forward, slipped again, and started scrambling for my life straight up the bluff. I couldn't stop until I reached a handhold or I would start sliding and never stop. The handhold came in the form of an overhang that I used as an anchor until I felt rested enough to pull myself up and over it. The rest of the climb was easy.

From atop the bluff, within the shelter of the pines, I saw an enormous blue lake stretching from north to south and east to west as far as I could see. At first, exhilarated by the climb and the view, I could only stand there congratulating myself for having made it that far. Then I watched the tower of clouds reach the sun and blot it out, and my exhilaration began to fade. I felt a chill bite of wind as the waters of the lake turned black, then frothed white. I realized just how big the lake was—far too big for Rupert and me to tackle it alone. Looking down the granite slope, which rose like one giant black wave curling in upon me, I knew I'd failed, and fought the urge to let go and ride the rock to the water below. A moment later, as Rupert reached the crest by a slower, safer route, I put that urge behind me.

"Well?" Rupert asked when we were safely back in the canoe.

"You're right. It's time to go home."

"You're sure?"

"I'm sure. That lake is too big for the two of us to cover, even if we had until spring, which we don't."

"What if we called in the authorities?"

I shrugged, unable at that moment to care one way or another. "What can they do that we haven't? Besides, we have more reason for finding Diana than they do."

"So what do you want to do?"

"Go home. Like I said."

"And leave Diana to John Knight?"

Taking a moment to pull myself together, I answered, "No. Like you said, we'll have to tell somebody up here. But I'd rather the world didn't know about it."

Rupert pulled on his rain suit and adjusted his hat. "Why don't you leave that up to me."

Over an hour later I left Rupert at the portage into Wild Horse Lake and went on in to John Knight's cabin alone. Though the day was somber and the waters dark, just as they had been my first trip there, I didn't have the same feeling of doom hanging over me. Nor did I find John Knight's cabin as stark, or his skinning shed as foul.

After gathering up Diana's things and putting them into the canoe, I took a walk to see what I might have missed. Nothing revealed itself to point me in a direction I hadn't already gone. The skinning shed still repelled and fascinated me as much as John Knight's house along Lost Road. Both were designed and erected by the same unsteady mind—made grotesque on purpose as if to serve an even more hideous purpose, and making me wonder what that purpose was.

"Satisfied?" Rupert asked on my return.

I looked back upon the black water of Wild Horse Lake. "Satisfied."

# 14

Dawn broke just as I was leaving the Bumble Bee Resort. Rupert had slept a couple of hours, then left in the night. I had some good-byes to say before I went.

The old man sat on the porch of his store watching the sun rise on Sand Lake. I stopped to watch it with him.

"So you're heading out, are you?" he said.

"Heading out," I answered.

"Are you sure you're doing the right thing?"

We watched the sun's first cool rays stripe the lake. "No. But at the moment it seems the only thing to do."

"I'll keep an eye out for John Knight," he promised. "I'm sure Patsy and the other locals will do the same."

A fish jumped, well out in the bay, making orange ripples in the water. "Is it always this beautiful here?" I asked.

"Always," he said, his old eyes bright with wonder. "You should have seen that storm coming down the lake the other day. Now, there was a sight to behold."

"I'll bet."

His eyes never wavered. He took it all in, as if it were his first time, or his last, to gaze upon Sand Lake. "They found a canoe washed up in Swanson's Bay yesterday," he said. "Somebody said it looked like Winter Knight's fishing rig."

"Where is Swanson's Bay?"

"Directly across the lake from Wild Horse Bay. But there's no telling where it drifted from."

"Were there any registration numbers on the canoe?"

He turned his gaze to me. He wanted to leave me with something, but he couldn't ignore the truth. "No. They couldn't find any."

"Isn't that unusual?"

"Maybe for you and me. Not for Winter Knight."

"Then are you saying it's his canoe?"

He smiled. "I won't know until I've had a look at it."

"Call me when you do."

I followed him into his store, where I intended to pay him whatever I owed him. But he wouldn't take any money. "Why not?" I asked.

"Because you remind me of someone I used to know. Me, about forty years ago." He handed me a sack containing a half-dozen doughnuts and a thermos of coffee. "Here," he said, "in case you get hungry along the way."

"I don't know what to say," I said.

"Why say anything."

Then I remembered something I'd wanted to ask

181

him. "When did John Knight build his skinning shed? Was it recently?"

He scratched his chin thoughtfully. "I don't recall he even had one, leastwise that I know of."

"Maybe I'm not describing it right," I said. "It's a long low building that sits in the woods above his cabin."

Again he drew a blank. "It's news to me," he said. "Winter inherited the cabin and the privy from the trapper he bought it off of. Then he built the workshop himself several years ago. But I don't know anything about that building you described." He used his cane to bounce his first ant of the day. "You see, Winter fancied himself a trapper, just like a lot of people with big boats and expensive gear fancy themselves fishermen, but the truth is he did more talking than trapping."

"Maybe he built it this summer," I suggested. "Didn't you say that some of the people flying over saw building going on there?"

"That they did," he agreed. His eyes clouded momentarily, then brightened again. "I am disappointed in Winter, though. He could have at least stuck his head in the door and said hello, seeing that he stopped by here regular in the past."

"He probably didn't want anyone to know he was back."

"That'd be my guess," he said, "seeing how things turned out."

I shook the old man's hand. "You're one in a million," I said. "Take care of yourself."

"I plan to," he said with a smile. "I plan to."

Minutes later I came to the fork in the road. To the right was Sand Lake and the Black Bear Lodge. To the left was Oakalla and the way home. I could picture the sun on Sand Lake, Patsy Bircher as she stood in her coffee shop, filling saltshakers and starting another morning. I could see a boy I used to know there with her, pumping gas, checking equipment, and readying the boats for another day's fishing. I could see him, after his day's work was done, bounding up the path to his cabin and back down again, a rod and reel in his hand and a smile on his face, as he met life head-on with the clear bright eyes of innocence. But try though I might, I couldn't see me.

I drove through Duluth-Superior, got on I-94 at Eau Claire, and continued south toward Oakalla. Ahead of me, the cold front that had passed through Sand Lake in the night continued to scoop up clouds like a bulldozer, rolling one dark billow upon another as they filled the sky. Soon I drove into a rain and stayed there all the way home.

Oakalla had never looked so good to me. Slowing to about walking speed, I noted every house along Jackson Street, every signpost, tree, and streetlight. I rolled down my window to take it all in, heard the puddles splash under Jessie's tires, smelled the lawns and the leaves and the smoke of someone's fire, felt myself relax, let go. Only then did I realize that for the first time in seven years I'd missed my deadline for the *Oakalla Reporter*.

Turning north at the five-and-dime, I parked Jessie in the garage, patted her rear fender, and gave her my heartfelt promise—soon, I knew, to be broken—never to doubt her again. Then I took a deep breath and went inside.

Ruth sat in her chair with a magazine in her lap and her eyes closed. I stood a moment, thinking she'd awaken. When she didn't I knelt by the hearth and poked around in the ashes, raising a cloud of dust that whitened my shoes.

"Welcome home," Ruth said.

I turned to look at her. She picked up her magazine, pretending to read. I put the poker down and sat on the hearth. Ruth put her magazine down and glanced around the room. We each wanted to hug the other, but neither would make the first move.

"So," she said, "how long are you home for?"

"For good," I answered. "At least as far as I know."

"Is that your head or your heart talking?"

"I'll let you know in the morning."

"Fair enough." She set the magazine to one side and stood up. "Now, do you want a cup of coffee or something stronger?"

"Something stronger."

She gave me one of her rare smiles. "In the buffet there's a pint of Southern Comfort that Aunt Emma gave me this spring. She said she doubted they'd let her have it in the hospital." Aunt Emma had gone into the hospital to dry out, but left after the first day because they wouldn't let her smoke in bed.

She got the glasses and poured us each two wide fingers worth of Southern Comfort. Normally a non-drinker, except for a weekly beer with her Sunday night popcorn, Ruth looked at her glass, looked at mine, then traded glasses with me when she saw I had the larger measure.

"Is there something we're celebrating?" I asked.

"Your homecoming."

"Besides that?"

"The *Oakalla Reporter*," she said proudly. "We made our deadline."

"We did!" I said, delighted. "Let me see it!"

She brought me a crisp white copy of that day's edition. I could tell she'd been saving it for me, because it hadn't been read yet. After glancing over the first

184

page and seeing nothing amiss, I said, "I'm impressed. I couldn't have done better myself."

She took a drink and set her glass down. I noticed her Southern Comfort was going faster than mine. "Maybe you'd better look through the rest of the paper," she said.

I looked through the rest of the paper, which, besides its usual number of advertisements, had been filled with letters to the editor. I didn't read the letters. My mind wasn't yet ready to absorb them. But I did note the advertisement for Heavin's Market. It read just as I'd written it. I wondered what Howard Heavin's reaction had been.

Meanwhile Ruth went into the kitchen and returned with a bushel basket full of mail, by far the most I'd ever gotten in a single week. "Some of these are like those I printed in the paper," she said. "We couldn't have printed all of them if we'd tried. The rest are letters to you about Diana, wishing you well and offering help and support." She took another drink of Southern Comfort. "You might want to read them sometime."

"How did they know about Diana?" I said, lifting a stack of letters from the basket and sorting through them.

"Evidently Sniffy Smith put the word out. If you look hard enough, you might even find one from Edna Pyle," she said with regret.

"What did Edna have to say?" I laid the letters back into the basket.

"Nothing that will stand up in court," she answered. "Though, I guess for her it was close to an apology."

"And did Howard Heavin call?" I asked.

"First thing this morning. He loved the ad you

**185**

wrote for him. But he said you'd probably better not do it again. Not if he wanted to keep his happy home."

I smiled. Some things never changed. Then I said, "How did the vote go?"

"What vote are you talking about?"

"Reality versus paranormal. Does anybody else in Oakalla have prophetic dreams like you do?"

She finished the rest of her Southern Comfort, stood, then wiped her mouth with the back of her hand on the way to the kitchen. I noticed she wobbled a little as she went. "Half the town does, if you can put any stock in what they say." I heard her rinse her glass in the sink and set it on the counter. "I don't."

"You think you're the only one, then?" I called. She didn't answer. "Ruth?"

"I heard you the first time," she called back.

When she said nothing further, I went into the kitchen, where she sat at the table and stared straight ahead into the wall. "Did I miss something?" I asked.

"You missed the fact that I haven't had a drink of hard liquor in over forty years, not since Karl came home from a Grange meeting and found me passed out in the bathtub. I've been trying for the past five minutes to get my legs to work, but you can see how far I've gotten."

"You want some help?"

"Not unless there's a wheelbarrow handy."

"I'll put some coffee on."

While standing at the stove, I noticed that Ruth's eyes were focused, even though the rest of her wasn't. She had fastened on something that wouldn't let go of her, even though she might have wanted it to. So, on the chance she might tell me, I said, "A penny for your thoughts?"

186

For once she didn't ignore me. "I know one place you haven't looked for Diana," she said.

"Where?" I forgot all about the coffee.

"The basement under John Knight's house on Lost Road."

"It doesn't have a basement."

She turned to me, her mind completely clear. "Yes, it does, Garth. At least it used to."

I sat down at the table across from her. "Tell me more."

She turned away to stare at the wall again. "Isn't that enough?"

"No, it's not enough," I said angrily. "Something's been eating at you ever since this whole business with Diana started. I think you owe it to me and yourself to tell the truth."

Turning back to me, she wore a don't-count-on-it look. "I gave you a direction. Why can't you leave it at that?"

"Because Diana is with John Knight somewhere in the north woods. So whatever you think is in that basement has more to do with you than me."

"Don't count on it," she said, meeting me eye to eye.

"Are you saying Diana might be there?" I couldn't believe that, no matter what Ruth said.

"I'm saying that place used to have a basement. Now it doesn't. It might do you good to find out why."

"No," I said.

She bristled. "What do you mean *no*?"

"I mean just that. I'm not going into that house again until you tell me why I should. What is there that you're afraid of?"

"Hattie McCorkle," she said before she could stop herself.

"Hattie McCorkle? The ghost of Lost Road?"

"Yes."

"How do you know she's there?"

She faced me squarely, like the trooper she was. "Because I put her there," she said. "With Esther McCorkle's help."

"Start at the beginning," I said. My own head had started to swim from too much Southern Comfort and too little sleep.

"There's no beginning to start at," she answered. "Hattie McCorkle was like a leech where Esther was concerned. Every time Esther and I would try to do something by ourselves, there she'd be, stuck so close to Esther's side, there'd be only one shadow. And it didn't do Esther any good to say something to Simon McCorkle either, because he just encouraged Hattie to tag along, afraid Esther might have some fun once she got out of his sight. So Esther hit upon a plan, one that I agreed to: We'd let Hattie follow us as far as the basement of McCorkle Chapel, where we'd lock her in for the day and maybe teach her a lesson."

"I thought Hattie was a simpleton." In which case it would be hard to teach her a lesson.

"She was. But now that I think about it, not nearly as simple as she let on, because she always seemed to know how to get her way."

"Where were you and Esther going?"

"Blackberry picking. At least that's what we told our folks. The truth of the matter is that we planned to go swimming in Rocky Creek."

"In the buff?" I asked.

She blushed. "Of course in the buff. It wouldn't have been any fun otherwise."

I rose and put on a pot of coffee. "Go on," I said.

"I forget where I was." Her eyes stared to glaze over.

"You and Esther were on your way to pick blackberries, or so your parents thought."

"That's right." She yawned. "But on the way we stopped by McCorkle Chapel and locked Hattie in the basement."

"How did you manage that?" I asked when she didn't continue.

She stared sleepily at me. "Easily enough. She saw us go into the church. She saw the basement door was open. She put two and two together and walked down the steps to the basement."

I turned down the fire under the coffee as Ruth laid her head on the table and closed her eyes. "Ruth?"

"I'm still here. But not for long."

"What happened after you locked Hattie in the basement of the church?"

"We went ahead and went swimming," she mumbled.

"Ruth?"

"Then I said I'd better stop and pick some blackberries or my folks might wonder. Esther said she didn't care if Simon McCorkle wondered or not. He was going to take the buggy whip to her anyway once he found out about Hattie. What about Hattie? I asked. Shouldn't we stop and let her out of the basement on the way home? No, she answered. A night in the church might do Hattie good . . ."

"Ruth, hang in there for a couple more minutes. It's important."

She lifted her head from the table and shook it, trying to clear cobwebs. "Then the storm blew in," she continued. "I was making a beeline for home when the lightning struck." Her eyes widened momentarily.

"One bolt, that's all it was. It dropped straight down out of the sky with a bang that set me back on my heels." Her voice began to trail off as her eyes closed once more. "By the time I reached McCorkle Chapel, it was already on fire. I tried to make myself go inside and see about Hattie, but once I got to the door, I couldn't go any farther. Too much fire in there," she mumbled. "Too much fire."

"Are you sure the lightning started the fire?" I asked.

"Yes."

"And that Hattie didn't somehow get out?"

She didn't answer. She'd fallen asleep.

After turning off the fire under the coffee, I helped Ruth up the stairs and into her bed where she bade me a groggy good night. Downstairs I poured myself a cup of coffee and sat down in my easy chair to think about all that had happened since Diana had called to tell me she was headed up north with Devin LeMay. But like Ruth, I couldn't keep my eyes open, and soon fell asleep.

# 15

It was still dark when I stumbled down the stairs the next morning to find Ruth with one hand on the back door and the other on the woodwork, steadying herself. I didn't know how long she'd been standing there. She was already dressed and had her purse slung over her shoulder.

"Were you going somewhere?" I asked.

"I don't see how that's any business of yours," she replied.

"I just thought you might want company."

"Not where I'm going," she said. "This is one trip I've got to make alone."

"We'll see," I answered.

I helped her into the kitchen, where she sat with her coat on and her purse hanging at her elbow. I poured us each a cup of coffee, then a second cup when we finished that. "You have any idea when you'll be back?" I asked.

"I thought you were going along."

"You said you didn't want company."

Holding her cup in both hands, she leaned over it to let the steam warm her face. "I changed my mind."

"Let me get dressed."

The rain had stopped in the night and the sky had cleared, leaving Oakalla's streets and sidewalks freshly washed, its lawns beaded and glistening. We went in Ruth's Volkswagen. She drove. I rode shotgun. In the trunk were a hammer, cat's-paw, wrecking bar, and shovel. We had the streets of Oakalla and then Fair Haven Road and all points west to ourselves, as we putted and jogged through the green-and-gold countryside.

"Feeling any better?" I asked.

"Some," she replied. "Ask me again in a week."

"Did you really think I wasn't going to make it back from up north?" I asked.

She wouldn't look at me. "I had my doubts. But when I heard that rattletrap of yours pull in last night, I felt something lift off my shoulders."

"Didn't Rupert tell you I'd be home soon?"

"Yes. But I didn't believe it."

"Why not?"

"Because I know how stubborn you are," she answered.

"No other reason?"

She didn't want to talk about it. "I still felt your danger."

"Did you happen to see the shape of it?"

She shook her head no.

We turned onto Lost Road and stopped in front of John Knight's house. Dark and opaque, it still glared at me with its hollow-eyed windows, like a thing alive. Massive, yet dwarflike in its deformity, the white oak still cast a wide shadow as chill as it was deep. Tangles of greenbrier and blackberry still rose up to block our entrance.

Ruth and I looked at each other at the same time. "Are you sure you want to do this?" she asked.

"I was about to ask you the same thing."

"We might as well," she said. "We've already come this far."

Inside the house we were stopped by the faint odor of death that had spread, since my last visit, to meet us at the door. Thick and sickly sweet, it caught in my throat and stayed there, a tickle I could neither cough up nor swallow. We went on. The smell of death stayed with us, neither gaining nor losing strength, as if it had permeated every pore of the house, then oozed out whenever the house breathed.

We came into the kitchen, where a fat black spider sat in his web over the table. Seeing the table set for a dinner for two, Ruth recoiled the same way I had when I first saw it.

"You didn't tell me this was here," she said.

"You never asked."

"I'm ready to get out. I don't like the feel of this place at all."

"I can't say I do either."

She looked at me with fear in her eyes. Something had really spooked her. "You don't understand, Garth," she said. "What you feel and what I feel are two different things. You see through your mind's eye and with your senses. You see and feel things as they are. I see and feel things as they were, and what happened here is too horrible for words. I can hardly stand to be in here."

"I don't imagine burning to death *was* much fun for Hattie McCorkle," I said.

"No. It's more than that," she answered.

"Can you describe it?"

"No. I don't think so."

She shuddered. It seemed her chill went bone-deep. "Can you go on?" I asked.

"I'd rather not."

"Then wait for me in the car."

"I'm sorry, Garth," she said. "But you can't know until you've been there."

"In that case I hope I never go there."

Ruth left. I waited to make sure she got out of the house okay, then went into John Knight's bedroom. It, too, wore the scent of death, perhaps more sharply than anywhere else in the house, as if the smell had run downhill with the house and pooled there. The two sleeping bags lay zipped together on the mattress as if someone had deliberately arranged them that way. They reminded me of the table set for two, and even of the pike's head and the bear trap hung on the front of John Knight's skinning shed—decorations for a desired effect, rather than accidental pairings.

I noticed Helen Carter Lemay's suitcase was gone. Had I not laid hands on it, felt its heft, and looked inside, I'd have wondered if I'd ever seen it to begin with.

The soft wooden floor of the bedroom bounced underfoot as I walked from corner to corner looking for a place to start. Finally I found a loose board that I could pry up with the wrecking bar, and after removing the nails so I wouldn't step on them, I shone my flashlight under the house and saw a stone stairway a few feet away. With one board already out, other boards came up easily, and it didn't take me long to get to the stairs.

I took the steps one at a time, making sure I didn't stub my toe on their rough surfaces. At the bottom looking up, I saw the charred beams of McCorkle Chapel, bent like black bones under the weight of the house. I wondered how the house had stood as long as it had. Even as I surveyed it, I heard its beams creak in the wind.

Curled, as if cold, a skeleton lay in the southwest corner of the basement. The bones and skull of another skeleton were scattered about the basement, as if something had rearranged them. I picked up the skull. Cracks led from the hole in the back of it like ice fissures on a pond. Gnawed and splintered, their marrow licked clean, the bones looked as though they'd been chewed on by something. Why, I wondered, had that something left the other skeleton untouched? And why, if it was the skeleton of Hattie McCorkle, was she wearing a wedding band?

Ruth sat in the Volkswagen. She looked better than when she'd left the house, but not by much. Then I noticed she'd been crying. I could only stand there and stare. In the seven years I'd known her I'd never seen her cry before.

"Are you all right?" I asked.

She nodded. "I can't explain what got into me, Garth, but there's a terrible sadness and betrayal here, as well as pain. I felt like it was happening to me."

"Maybe you just needed a good cry," I suggested.

She scowled at me. "And maybe you need to read what you write sometime. There are things that happen that we don't understand. Just because they haven't happened to you doesn't mean they aren't so. I thought you understood that."

"I'm trying to, Ruth. But sometimes it's hard."

"Well, try a little harder next time."

195

"Then tell me what I found under the house," I said, "if you're so attuned to me."

"I don't know what you found under the house, and I don't care," she replied. "I know what I feel, and whatever it is you found, it's not good."

"You're right," I agreed. "It's not good."

"Then why won't you believe me?"

"I believe you, Ruth. Up to a point."

"Which is?"

I shook my head in frustration. "I don't know. Like you said, my mind doesn't work the same way yours does. I can't accept what I haven't seen with my own two eyes. It's that simple."

"Which makes me what, a liar?" She was ready to do battle.

"No. I said I believed you."

"Up to a point, you said."

"Well, we've reached that point. That's why I want you to drive back to Oakalla and get Doc Airhart for me. Rupert, too, if he's around."

She balked at that. "I'll send them out here if you like, but once I get gone from here, I'm not coming back."

"Do as you like," I said. "Tell them I'll be waiting."

"Why can't you tell them yourself?"

"Because I need time to think, and here is as good a place as any to do it. Besides, having come this far, I don't want to go back to square one again."

"Why? Whatever you found won't walk away on you."

"No. But someone might carry it," I said, recalling Helen Carter LeMay's missing suitcase.

She glanced up and down Lost Road to make her point. "And who might that be way out here?"

For lack of a good answer, I said, "The last of the McCorkles." Little did I know how right I was.

After Ruth left, I walked back to the old McCorkle Cemetery to think. Once more encountering the low mounds there, I went back after the shovel and dug into one of them. Disappointed that I didn't find anything, I dug into another and again came up empty.

Doc Airhart turned around in Lost Road, parked his old black Cadillac in front of the house, and whistled for me.

"Coming!" I shouted.

A small man with white hair, an impish smile, and merry blue eyes, Doc Airhart kept all of us in Oakalla young with his energy and wit that seemed to sharpen with age. The year I moved to Oakalla, he'd retired at age seventy-five to devote more time to his yard and garden. But he'd recently admitted to me that he might have made a mistake, that there was only so much yard work and gardening he could do in a year's time before he started repeating himself. He wasn't complaining, mind you, but after fifty years of practicing medicine, he had a hard time getting excited about raising broccoli.

"Where's Rupert?" I asked.

He got out of the Cadillac and dusted himself off. "I don't know. It's not my day to watch him."

"Will he be along later?"

He shook his head. "Nope. Elvira said he had to drive over to Minneapolis to deliver a prisoner. She doesn't expect him back until late tonight." Noticing the house for the first time, he exclaimed, "Whew! Who built that thing?"

"A man by the name of John Knight."

He cocked his head to stare at it. "That's about the poorest excuse for a house I've ever seen. It makes my eyes water just looking at it."

"Wait'll you see what's inside," I said.

"No more bones, I hope."

"Ask me no questions . . ."

"Garth, you've dug up more than your share lately."

"Only Colonel Brainard's," I reminded him.

"What about Walter Lawrence?"

"That was Rupert and Clarkie. I was only the middleman."

Doc followed me through the briers toward the house. Stopping to study the white oak on the way, he clucked in confirmation, as he used to do when he diagnosed the ailment you thought would surely baffle him.

"You ever thought of airing out this place?" he asked once we were inside the house.

"What does it smell like to you?" I asked.

"Just what it smells like to you," he answered. "Like somebody died here."

"I didn't notice it as much a week ago when I was here."

"Probably a change in the weather. On some days you can smell better than others." I led him down to the basement, where he took a long look and said, "You'd better leave me for now, Garth." The tone of his voice said he'd already seen too much.

"What am I missing?" I asked. "All I see are bones."

Doc gave me a forgiving smile. "Sometimes there's comfort in ignorance."

I went upstairs and outside again, amusing myself by trying to stone the flying grasshoppers that landed in the dust along Lost Road. When I grew tired of that, I went to the white oak to examine the lightning scar that I'd discovered my first time there. If it and the tree were as old as I believed they were, then maybe Ruth had been wrong in blaming herself for Hattie McCorkle's death all those years. And maybe, had she faced the truth then, neither one of us would be facing it now.

Doc Airhart emerged from the house. His face as white as his hair, he looked dazed, unable to find the words for what he'd just seen.

"Doc?" I said.

He shook his head and handed me his keys. We drove in silence through the warm September afternoon. Light blue and mellow, crisscrossed with shadows, it seemed to wait upon him as I did. But he didn't speak until we pulled into his garage and closed the door behind us.

"I could use a drink," he said. "How about you?"

"Make mine a beer."

Doc returned with a water glass half-full of Scotch for him and a can of Old Style for me. "That's the nearest thing to a beer I have," he said.

"It'll do," I answered.

We sat on Doc's porch swing, swinging occasionally, watching the cars pass by the United Methodist Church on their way to and from town. Neither spoke for a long time. Doc was intent on collecting his thoughts. I was busy counting birthdays, trying to remember what had happened to me when. But try though I might, I couldn't recall Diana's face, or what was said the last time we made love.

"I've never seen anything quite like it, Garth," Doc said at last. "That's why it's so hard to come to grips with it."

"I thought you'd seen it all in your day."

He smiled for the first time since we left John Knight's house. "So did I, until today. But that beats all . . ." He turned to me. "She starved to death,

199

Garth. And she couldn't have been much over twenty years old."

"How about twelve years old?"

"No. She was a woman, not a child. She had her full growth in, at least before she started to starve."

From somewhere I could smell apples fermenting. "You're sure?" I asked.

"Dead sure," he said without a smile.

"What about the other set of bones?" I asked.

"I'd guess they came from a man in his thirties. Something had caved his skull in, so I guess that's how he died."

"He didn't starve to death?"

"No. He was murdered."

"Before or after the woman starved to death?"

Doc pushed off with his feet, swinging us to and fro a few times. When we'd coasted to a stop, he said, "Before."

"How long before?"

"Right before." His eyes were fixed on something straight ahead. "She fed off his body, Garth. No animal picked those bones clean."

I felt the rock in my stomach hit bottom. "Is that something we need to share with everyone?" I asked.

"Not on my account we don't."

"Do you have any idea how long ago it happened?"

"Not that long ago," he said.

"You mean it's not ancient history?"

He turned to me, his eyes regaining some of their sparkle. "I mean it's within the past ten years."

"How about the past four years?" Which was how long John Knight's house had been there.

"It's possible," he agreed. "I only said ten to cut myself some slack."

200

I rose from the swing. My legs felt a little wobbly. "Thanks, Doc. Sorry to put you through this."

"You didn't finish your beer," he said, picking up my can and setting it down again.

"I know. I'm trying to keep a clear head."

He took a drink of his Scotch. "I'm trying to muddle mine a little. Eighty-two years I've been at this business of life, and I had to pick today to be home." He smiled, remembering. "But then Constance said I never did have any luck."

"Yeah. I know the feeling." Taking my rock with me, I left.

"What do you mean Hattie wasn't under there?" Ruth said on my return home. "She had to be."

"Doc said she wasn't." I'd gone as far as to tell Ruth the ages and sexes of the skeletons I'd found, but not what had happened to them.

"What does that old quack know?" she said.

"He spent five years as Cayahoga County coroner before he came here. And he was county coroner most of the years he was practicing here."

"I know all that," she said, banging a skillet down on the stove. "I'm the one who told you."

"So why don't you believe him?"

"Because Hattie McCorkle died in that fire!" she insisted. "I saw the church burn down on top of her."

"I searched the basement myself," I said. "Hattie McCorkle wasn't there."

"Then who was there? Tell me that." She flattened a hamburger patty and threw it into the skillet.

"I don't know for sure," I said. "But Helen Carter LeMay is one guess."

She glanced sharply at me. "Devin LeMay's wife?"

"And John Knight's lover," I added.

Ruth threw another hamburger patty into the skil-

201

let beside the first, salted and peppered them, then sliced an onion and a tomato. "If one is Helen Carter LeMay," she said on her way to the refrigerator, "who, then, is the other one?"

"I don't know," I said. "Unless we find John Knight, I doubt we'll ever know."

Her hand was on the refrigerator door when she turned around to face me, wearing a triumphant look.

"I know who it might be," she said.

"Who?"

She told me.

In the moments that followed, when I could finally get my brain to work long enough to put all the pieces of the puzzle together, I knew she was right.

"I think I know where Diana is," I said.

After a call to Orley, then to Sand Lake, Minnesota, I knew for sure.

# 16

*I*'d parked Jessie in a patch of woods where it would take more than a casual glance to see her, then made the long walk down to the lake where the moon shone as a white sliver, a day away from no moon at all. Wearing jeans, dark-blue socks, and a T-shirt, and soiled gray tennis shoes, I waited among the shadows.

A soft warm breeze blew off Lake Mendota, brought the smell of fish and gasoline, the *put-put-put* of a cabin cruiser, and the mumble of faraway voices. A katydid sang nearby. Six more weeks until the first frost, Grandmother Ryland would say.

Devin LeMay's bedroom light was on, but I doubted he was in bed. It seemed as though day in and day out he needed very little sleep and only an occasional meal to survive, as though he fed off of his own inertia for as long as he could, then collapsed until a new surge of energy propelled him on his way again.

He'd slept little at Sand Lake the last night he was there, but with a few days at home to catch up, he would be his old self again.

Who was Devin LeMay? I didn't know, doubted if anyone ever had known or would know exactly how his mind worked. I knew he was the last of the McCorkles, in spirit at least, if not in flesh, that he'd starved his wife and mother to death, killed his wife's lover, kidnapped Diana, and twice tried to kill me. He'd built the skinning shed on Wild Horse Lake and the house on Lost Road. Both were intended as death houses, one for John Knight and the other for me. But he'd fallen into his own trap on Wild Horse Lake and had to chop his way out, which left a way open for me to escape. John Knight, however, wasn't so lucky. Those were his bones we'd found under the house on Lost Road, his body that fed Helen Carter LeMay until it, too, was consumed, along with her.

I wondered at what point in each of their lives those who loved and trusted Devin LeMay realized the truth about him—that instead of the lamb or the shepherd, he was the wolf in sheep's clothing. Perhaps his mother never knew that much, perhaps she knew only that the meals delivered to her room stopped one day and never started again. John Knight perhaps knew at the instant of his death, but he never had the chance to act on that knowledge. Helen Carter LeMay had far too long to know and dwell upon it. Diana less time.

But of them all, I felt the sorriest for Esther Mc-Corkle, who had taken Devin LeMay and his mother into her home as family and raised him as her own grandson. Her discovery had driven her to suicide, and as the waters of Lake Mendota closed in over her, she must have wondered what she had ever done to deserve a father like Simon McCorkle and a child like Devin LeMay.

Wearing only her white terry robe, Jenny Carter came out her front door, crossed from her adjoining yard over into Devin LeMay's, and walked out onto his pier. Almost defiantly, as if she knew he were watching from his bedroom window, she took off her robe, turned toward the house, and held her pose momentarily before diving into the lake.

I wanted to like Jenny Carter, wanted to think she was a victim of Devin LeMay, as John Knight had been—not without blemish and certainly not without guilt, but not evil at heart. Yet of the two I felt more compassion for John Knight.

Entering Devin LeMay's boathouse, I took what I needed, took off my shoes and socks, and slipped under the pier, working my way out toward deep water. Jenny Carter swam in close to the pier. I stretched out the ski harness and waited, but she drifted away again.

Perhaps Jenny had done what she had done out of a fear of Devin LeMay. Perhaps she knew better than anyone that he wasn't the ingratiating weakling, or the boyish bumbler that he pretended to be. He used those weights up in his bedroom. They weren't just there for decoration. He also knew how to use a hammer and saw, and could handle a speedboat as well as anyone I'd ever met.

Twice he'd tried to kill me. The first time was in the storm on Wild Horse Bay. The second time was the next day when he upset the canoe and tried "accidentally" to drown me. Looking back on it, I doubted that he'd thrown my sandwich overboard accidentally either, but had done so, despite his apologetic shrug, out of malice.

I should have paid more attention to that first night

on Sand Lake when I saw him land the boat so expertly, then jump to the pier with the grace of a cat; or to that second night on my way to the dump when someone followed me so skillfully and stealthily without my ever knowing who it was. No bumbler, or weakling, could have done those things, or any of the other things he had accomplished, such as building the skinning shed there on Wild Horse Lake. The man who had accomplished them was clever, resourceful, strong, and agile, in mind and body—and a consummate actor. With that knowledge, Jenny Carter had every reason to fear him.

But the cynic in me said that Jenny Carter enjoyed her role in Devin LeMay's life, and had he given her an even larger role to play, she would have played it willingly. She had betrayed her own sister by acting as Devin LeMay's spy and telling him of Helen's plans to run away with John Knight. She had called Ned Emery, pretending to be a fur buyer, and thus established the fact that John Knight was still alive. She had kept Diana captive in her house, then turned my thoughts elsewhere there in the attic when I got too close to the truth. She had posed as Diana for the old man at the Bumble Bee Resort, then returned home by bus from Orley, Minnesota, the next day. She'd made the phone calls to the Madison police on cue, then fed me all the right information, which led me to Ned Emery, which led me to John Knight and Wild Horse Lake, where Devin LeMay's trap was set and baited. Ironically, the wind must have blown the door closed on him as it had on me, and he'd lost precious time and advantage while chopping himself out, which explained his frantic phone call home from the Black Bear Lodge in the middle of the night. However, Jenny must have then assured him that I was on my way, and with a little more patience on his part, he could still make his plan work. For that reason alone Jenny Carter deserved whatever she had coming.

She swam toward me in long easy strokes, glided in close, and was reaching for the pier when I surfaced behind her. Something told her I was there. She hurriedly grasped the side and tried to throw herself onto the pier. But before she could reach safety, I looped the ski harness around her throat.

Dragging her back down into the water, I tightened the harness and held on. Not one to go quietly, Jenny arched, bucked, thrashed, and kicked until I was afraid she'd attract someone's attention. I leaned into her and caught an elbow in the ribs, followed by another. As I tightened my grip even more, I feared I might kill her before she would ever stop struggling. I didn't want that. Neither did I want Devin LeMay to hear us.

Moments later I dragged her unconscious body into shallow water next to the pier, made sure she was still breathing, and tied her with the ski rope. Then I set her down in the water and waited. Somewhere across the lake a dog barked. It sounded like laughter to me.

She awakened with a gasp, followed by an aborted scream that I cut short with the ski rope. "Try that again, Jenny, and you won't wake up next time."

"Who are you?"

"Garth Ryland. Weren't you expecting me?"

She stiffened. "*You*," she said hoarsely. "I told Devin you'd be back, that he'd better be careful. But he just laughed at me."

I waited for a boat to pass, its light trailing a red streamer through the water. Jenny Carter gathered herself, weighing her chances. I sawed the ski harness across her throat to remind her of my promise. She relaxed, as the boat went on. Then Devin LeMay's

**207**

bedroom light went out. Just a few more minutes, I told myself.

"How long have you been sleeping with Devin LeMay?" I asked.

"What business is that of yours?"

Tightening the harness, I asked again. "How long, Jenny?"

"Since I was fourteen or fifteen. But it doesn't matter. He loves me. He's always loved me." She screwed her head around to look at me. Hatred in its purest form showed in her eyes. "Something you wouldn't understand."

"Probably not," I said. "But there are a lot of things I don't understand."

"Like Devin and Diana?" she said with a smirk.

"Among other things," I said.

"Do you want to know what they did in his bed?" she taunted. "Devin told me, you know. He tells me *everything*."

"If you can bear to tell it," I said, "I can bear to listen."

"I hate you!" she hissed, trying to spit on me.

"I know that. Now tell me the truth about what happened to Devin's mother."

She turned away to look at Devin LeMay's darkened house. Something in her crumbled as she did. "I told you what happened to Devin's mother," she said weakly. "She starved herself to death."

"Isn't it the other way around? Didn't Devin starve her to death after Esther McCorkle died?"

"No!" she cried, fighting back tears. "That wasn't the way it happened at all. He loved his mother. He . . ." She stopped, unable to preserve the lie.

"He killed her, slowly, a day at a time," I said.

"Yes," she admitted. "He did. But not right away."

She still felt the need to defend him. "He didn't starve her right away. It was only after she had a stroke and got bedfast."

"She didn't have a stroke, Jenny. He just got tired of feeding her."

"But he tried!" she insisted. "He really tried for two or three years. But then it just got too much for him."

"Who had his mother's room built without windows, Devin or Esther McCorkle?"

"She must have. It's been that way as long as I can remember."

"Why? Do you know?"

"No. Something to do with his mother, but not even Devin knew what it was. Devin wondered if she might have been a criminal or something, the way his grandmother always kept her shut in."

"You know, don't you, that Esther McCorkle wasn't really Devin's grandmother?" I watched the lights across the lake blink off one by one. "Esther McCorkle's only child died over fifty years ago."

"That's not true," she answered.

"It is true, Jenny. Whoever Devin LeMay is, he's not Esther McCorkle's grandson."

"Don't tell Devin that," she said with a worried look. "It'll kill him."

I studied her. No, Jenny Carter didn't see the irony of her last statement. "Is Diana still alive?" I asked her.

She hesitated. I'd caught her off guard, which was my intention. "What if I say no?" she asked.

"Then I'll throw you off the end of the pier."

"That'd be murder," she insisted.

"So it would be. But who would ever know who did it?"

"Devin would."

I didn't answer. The silence made her squirm.

**209**

"He *would*," she repeated. "Then he'd make you pay."

"If you go off the end of the pier," I said evenly, "Devin LeMay goes with you."

"I'd like to see that." She laughed.

I tightened the ski harness around her throat, choking off her laughter. "Too bad you won't."

"You can't scare me," she whispered, once she got her voice back.

"I'm not trying to scare you, Jenny. I asked you a question, and I want an answer. Is Diana still alive?"

"Yes," she replied. "She's still alive."

"In Devin's mother's room?"

"Yes, I think so. He hasn't let me in the house since he's been home."

"You kept her for him, didn't you, in your basement?"

"Yes. In the coal bin. Then Devin made me scrub it out afterward," she said angrily. "And clean her up, too."

"One last question, Jenny," I said. "Where does he keep the key to his mother's bedroom?"

"If I tell you?" she asked.

"You go on living."

"And Devin? What will you do to him?" she demanded.

"I don't care about Devin. All I want is Diana."

"You'd just let him go after all he's done?" Even Jenny Carter found that hard to believe.

"No. Not let him go. I'll have to tell the police what I know."

"They won't believe you. Everybody who knows him loves Devin," she said proudly.

"Then you have nothing to worry about."

She thought it over. The moon had passed the

**210**

meridian and hung hangnail-thin over the waters of Lake Mendota. No boats were in sight. The moon had the lake to itself.

"There's a loose brick above the fireplace," Jenny said. "The key is behind it."

"Any chance he's moved it?"

"No," she said, subdued. "No chance at all."

She didn't resist when I gagged her with the belt from her terry robe and set her with her back against the seawall. Chest-deep in water, she had two choices— struggle and risk drowning, or sit quietly until someone untied her. For her sake I hoped she made the right one.

# 17

*I* found the key where Jenny said it would be and made my way along the hall toward the room where Diana was kept prisoner. The house seemed too quiet to me, as though it watched on tiptoes for something to happen. Every step, every creak of the floorboards, was muted, until, in the waiting silence, I could hear the lap of Lake Mendota on the seawall outside.

Unlocking Diana's door, then easing it closed as I went inside, I took a couple of steps and waited. When nothing happened, I took another step and stopped, then another and stopped again. My heart raced the way it did whenever I approached a dog on point, knowing something was about to jump out at me.

Too absorbed in Devin LeMay, I'd forgotten Diana's courage, how she'd once stepped in front of a loaded shotgun rather than risk my life for the sake of hers. I'd forgotten that Devin LeMay had fooled her not once, but twice, and she'd be damned if there would ever be a third time.

Diana rushed at me with a snarl, trying to dig out my eyes with her nails. I dropped the poker I carried and tried to ward her off as best I could without hurting her. Enraged and determined to do as much damage as she could while she had the advantage, she fought with a fury that would not be denied.

Escape never entered her mind. Not at the beginning when she bit my hand and raked the skin from my face. Not at the end when I had her pinned to the floor with all of my weight on top of her. She still tried to get at me, still fought with every ounce of her being to hurt him, who had so hurt her. I knew then why I had loved her at first sight and would always love her somewhere deep in my soul. Never had I met anyone with more life than she.

"*Diana,*" I whispered. "It's Garth.

"No!" She continued to struggle.

"*Yes.*"

She stopped, to feel my arms, then my face. "Oh, Garth!" She sighed. "It is you."

"Shh," I said, putting my finger to her lips. "I'd rather not let anyone else know that just yet."

I got off of her. We sat side by side on the floor, holding each other up. Together our breathing slowed and quieted, like those times that seemed so long in the past when we used to make love.

"I told him you'd come for me," she said. "That you wouldn't rest until you found me. Do you know what his answer was?"

" 'I know,' " I answered for her. "His answer was 'I know.' "

"*Yes,*" she said. "It sent a chill right through my heart."

"You were here all along?"

"Here, and next door in the basement." She pressed closer, resting her head against mine. "I had my hands tied behind my back, and a rag stuffed into my mouth, so all I could do was to keep kicking the door to the coal bin, hoping someone would hear. Then I thought I heard your voice outside and began kicking all the harder." When she spoke again, her tone was forlorn. "Then your voice went away, and I didn't have the heart to kick anymore."

"I was up in the attic looking for a bat."

"I know," she said angrily. "Jenny told me how she tricked you. She also told me something else. . . ." She stopped. The words caught in her throat.

"It didn't happen," I assured her. "I won't say I wasn't tempted, but it didn't happen." Then I said, "Where's the light in here? I forget."

"It's by the door. I'll get it."

The shock of seeing each other again almost proved too much for both of us. She wore a sheer lavender gown, a hint of makeup, which was all she ever needed, and the beginning of a bruise under her right eye, from our struggle. "Here," I said, taking her Indian bead necklace out of my pocket and putting it around her neck. "I'd like to see you with this on."

"It's hardly ever off," she said, caressing it. "Where did you find it?"

"It's not important."

"And when did you shave last?" she asked, rubbing my beard.

"I don't know. I've forgotten."

"You look good in it," she said.

A board creaked above us. Holding up my hand for silence, I asked, "How heavy a sleeper is Devin?"

"Heavy, when he sleeps," she answered.

"Somehow that's not reassuring."

She gave me her go-to-hell look. "You know what I mean."

"Here's what I want you to do," I said. "Leave by the back door and go to Jessie." I told her where Jessie was. "When you get there, wait for an hour. If I don't show up by then, go for help."

"What are you planning to do, Garth?" she asked.

"Leave that up to me," I said. "Now get going."

She dug in her heels. "Not without you, I'm not."

"Look," I said, not caring whether she liked it or not. "We've done it your way from the beginning. From the time you met Devin LeMay until now. From now on we're doing it my way."

"You plan to kill him, don't you?" she asked.

"Whatever I do to him or whatever he does to me, I don't want you around to see. But, no, I don't plan to kill him. Not if I don't have to anyway. So get going. We're wasting time."

"Garth . . ."

I cut her short. "I said get going. We can talk later."

"No, what if there's not a later?"

"There will be," I promised. Though I wasn't nearly as sure as I sounded.

She left. I took one last long look around the room that had been her prison. My eyes stopped on the framed yellow parchment above the mantel that was the original deed for the McCorkle homestead. It didn't read any easier than the first time I'd looked at it, but I judged Henry McCorkle was probably right about one thing: It did look as though Abraham Lincoln *had* signed the deed himself. Henry was also right in his judgment of the man who'd stolen the deed from him. "A wolf in sheep's clothing," he'd called him. Henry McCorkle knew his wolves.

Devin LeMay in his little blue-and-white sailor suit stood at attention beside his mother in her long lacy white dress. He appeared as competent, she as reclusive as ever. But there was something subtly wrong with the photograph that I still couldn't quite grasp. I wished Ruth were there to set me straight.

The stairs to Devin LeMay's room creaked twice on my way up them. At the door to his room I listened for any sound that might tell me where he was.

If he breathed, I couldn't hear him. If he moved at all, I couldn't feel the vibrations. Yet I knew he was there. Quiet, controlled, unrelenting, his presence bore down on me—as it had that day on Wild Horse Lake and that same night on the path to the dump—with all the weight of his malevolence. As my arms began to tremble, my legs cramped, and something deep inside me cried for mercy. Devin LeMay in and of himself wasn't much. His power came from his arrogance, and the McCorkle legacy, which allowed him to pursue his ends by any means without the encumbrance of conscience.

I opened the door. Diving across the threshold into his room, I rolled to a crouch and held the poker head-high to ward off any blows. I didn't hear the first disk from his weight set coming, only the clang of metal against metal, as the disk skimmed the poker, struck my face a glancing blow, and ricocheted into the wall. Another disk followed, burying itself with a thud into Devin LeMay's water bed. I scrambled to retrieve it. It felt like about five pounds of iron to me. That left him with only three hundred pounds or so.

A third disk, this one larger and heavier than the first two, slammed into the water bed beside me. Before I had time to retrieve it, a fourth caught me in the shoulder, knocking me back against the bed and leaving my left arm temporarily numb. In anger I whistled the second disk back his way and saw it smash into a mirror, as glass blew like dust.

Gathering the remaining weights in my right arm while scooting the poker on ahead of me, I moved along the length of the bed as quietly as I could. Without warning, a heavy disk, at least twenty-five pounds worth, came out of nowhere and landed flat on the carpet behind me. A second twenty-five pounder barely missed my head, landing with a concussion that shook the room.

I took a moment to think things over. In past boyhood games of combat that included apple, corncob, and snowball fights, I never won when I played it soft and tried to wait the others out. Invariably my teammates would fall off one by one until I'd end up alone and cornered; or I'd get hit with a lucky throw that put me out of the game. So I devised a strategy, like the fox with one trick, that almost always worked for me. With a spring and a shout, I charged like hell right into the teeth of the enemy.

Devin LeMay didn't expect me so soon. He barely had time to brace himself before I dived on top of him. Thinking they'd only slow me down, I'd fired the weights and poker at him in rapid succession, leaving him no time to respond. On top of him, with my fingers at his throat, I wished I'd kept the five-pound weight to smash into his face.

We rolled apart. I could hear and feel the glass from the mirror crunch under me. He found another disk, lifted it in both hands, and came toward me. I charged, aiming straight for the disk with my hands, so he wouldn't have a chance to swing it. The force of my charge carried him over backward with me on top, but he still held onto the disk, grinding it into my skull, as I burrowed into him to escape it.

I rose, lifted him off the carpet, and threw us both to the carpet again, driving my shoulder into his throat. Still he continued to saw at me with the weight. That wouldn't do for much longer. Already he'd ground his way through the layer of hair and scalp and hit bone.

I lifted him, higher than before, and literally tried to drive my shoulder through his throat as I slammed him to the floor. He dropped the weight. I lifted him again, slammed him, lifted, slammed, until I fell exhausted beside him. Lying there in the darkness, the lap of Lake Mendota a soothing lullaby, I could still hear Devin LeMay breathing.

In the time it took the earth to cool and the dinosaurs to disappear, I found the light to the bedroom and turned it on. Glass lay everywhere, glinted like tiny white eyes in the black carpet. Devin LeMay lay on his back with his eyes closed. His face unmarked, his arms stretched leisurely out at his side, he appeared to be merely catnapping.

I glanced at myself in one of the mirrors. Bruised in several places and spattered with my own blood, I looked like I had a bad case of chicken pox. I felt the furrow in my head that Devin LeMay had cut with the disk. Three or four inches long and deep enough to plant corn, it burned more than it bled, though it was doing a good job of both.

Gathering up the smaller weights, I began smashing mirrors, saving the mirrored ceiling for last. I picked up a ten-pound disk, curled my arm around it, and with a hop and whirl hurled it upward. I didn't close my eyes. I wanted to see the glass rain down on Devin LeMay.

I could have opened the skylight with my hands. I

used a disk instead. Lifting Devin LeMay onto my shoulder, I climbed up on a chair and stuffed him through the hole in the skylight. Perhaps the fall from his roof wouldn't kill him. Perhaps it would only break his back or his neck and leave him paralyzed the rest of his life. Poetic justice either way.

But once I had him on the roof, I had a hard time getting my own shoulders through the hole. I began to chip at the hole with a weight, but the longer I chipped, the less I felt like chipping. I searched my soul and knew I was about to make the biggest mistake of my life. Then I reached up through the hole and dragged Devin LeMay back to earth again.

# 18

*I* emptied the last of the gallon of gasoline. Though the smell of it was everywhere around me, in every crack and crevice, I could still smell death oozing out of the house along Lost Road. Then I called Ruth over to the white oak that shadowed the entrance to the house. "Come here, I want to show you something," I said.

Reluctantly she got out of Jessie and came over to me. "This better be important," she said. "I didn't want to come along in the first place."

Pointing to the lightning scar, illumined by my flashlight, I asked, "What do you think?"

"What do I think about what?"

"The lightning scar. You have to admit it's old, nearly as old as the tree itself."

"Which proves what?" She was losing patience

with me. "And don't beat around the bush, because I'm not in the mood."

"It might prove that lightning struck this tree instead of McCorkle Chapel like you thought. That the fire you saw wasn't caused by lightning, but deliberately set by Esther McCorkle to kill her sister, Hattie."

Ruth stared stonily at me, then nodded to herself in understanding. "So that's what this is all about."

"Then it could have happened that way?" I was full of hope.

She patted me on the shoulder as she walked past on her way to Jessie. "No, Garth, it couldn't have. But thanks anyway for trying."

"Why couldn't it have happened that way?" I asked a few minutes later. We'd stopped at the end of Lost Road to watch the fire burn. It carved a red dome in the night, made the stars disappear.

"Two reasons," she said, watching the fire. "One is that no matter how she might have felt about her sister, I doubt if Esther would have set out to deliberately kill her. Hattie was no threat to her. A nuisance, for sure, but no threat. Besides, I don't think Esther was capable of murdering anyone in cold blood. Though I do wonder about her and Simon."

I watched the fire reach its crest, then begin to fall. For all of its history the house burned like any other, neither brighter, nor longer, nor hotter. "Why do you wonder about her and Simon?" I asked.

"Karl. He was on his way over to help Simon put up hay when he saw Esther carry a board out into the woods and hide it." She watched the fire fall farther until it just cleared the tops of the trees. "Karl's the one who found Simon hanging on the hay hook with splinters sticking out of the knot on his head. He later asked me if he should say anything about seeing Esther with the board."

"What did you tell him?"

"I told him to let his conscience be his guide. But as far as I was concerned, Esther had already suffered enough at Simon's hands. She didn't owe him the rest of her life."

"Good point," I agreed.

"Seen enough?" Ruth asked.

I started Jessie. "Yes. I've seen enough."

"But I've always wondered," she continued, "what finally drove Esther to it. She'd put up with Simon all those years, more years than I have in me, and then one day she killed him. Why, Garth? And how did she ever get him hung up on that hay hook by herself? Answer me that, and maybe I'll start sleeping better at night."

"I wish I could," I said.

We left Lost Road and the fire behind us as the stars came out again. Leaning out my window as the sweet September night rushed in at me, I counted as many stars as I could. "What's your second reason?" I asked.

"My second reason for what?"

"For thinking that lightning struck the church instead of the tree."

"That's easy enough to answer," she said. "Lightning struck the tree the year before and killed one of Pop's horses and left the other a little loony for the rest of his life. Pop was working in McCorkle Chapel when it happened, helping to dig the basement."

"That's it, Ruth!" I said, pounding my hand on Jessie's steering wheel. "That's where those mounds came from in the McCorkle Cemetery. That's the dirt and debris Devin LeMay carried out of the basement when he cleared it."

222

"And likely Hattie McCorkle's bones along with it," she said, resigned.

"Maybe not," I said. "I didn't find any when I dug through a couple of those mounds."

"That doesn't mean they're not there."

"No," I agreed, knowing I'd left several mounds unopened.

After parking Jessie in the garage, I got out and started up the alley. Ruth got out and headed for the house. "Where are you going?" she asked.

"It's a nice night. I thought I'd take a walk."

"Is that all you're doing?" She was disappointed in me. She already knew where I was going.

"You never know," I answered. She shrugged and went on. I waited until she'd almost reached the door before I said, "Ruth, do you feel any different?"

"About what?"

"The house. Do you feel any different now that we've burned it down?"

"No. Why should I?"

"No reason, I guess. I just thought you might suddenly feel a lot lighter."

"Like an eagle-sized burden just lifted off my shoulders?"

"Yeah. I guess that's it."

"I'm sorry, Garth. It doesn't always work that way."

"Win some, lose some," I replied.

She went on into the house. I went on up the alley.

A few minutes later I rang Diana's doorbell. She came to the door barefoot, wearing jeans and a University of Wisconsin sweatshirt, her hair tied up in a knot. She looked lovely. Even on her worst days, and that appeared to have been one of them, I'd never seen her look anything else.

"I wasn't expecting you," she said from within my arms.

"I wasn't expecting me either. Do you mind if I come in?"

She stepped back, saw what was in my eyes and on my mind. "Sure. Come on in."

I followed her into the kitchen, where she was packing her things into cardboard boxes. "Can I get you anything?" she asked.

"No, thanks."

"Should I get me anything?"

I smiled at her. "Why don't you bring us both a beer."

She did, then sat at the table beside me. Free and easy, completely disarmed, it felt like us at the beginning, when we were just friends.

"I suppose this is good-bye," she said.

"I suppose it is," I answered.

We drank our beer in silence and listened to the grandfather clock in the parlor tick away the minutes. From somewhere a late-summer breeze found its way into the kitchen and brought a bushel of memories with it. I looked at Diana at the same time she looked at me. Then she smiled at me. I loved her smile. It was mischief itself. "Like old times," she said.

"Real old times," I pointed out.

She nodded in understanding. "I was thinking about that at Devin's. Locked in that room, there wasn't much else to do but think. We lost something after Fran died. I want to say our friendship."

"Why not say it?" I asked. "I feel the same way."

"But we *were* the best of friends," she said. "Why not make love to each other? It was something we both wanted, and had wanted for a long time. Best friends should make the best lovers."

224

"I know," I agreed.

"Then where did we go wrong?"

"I don't know that we did go wrong," I answered. "Maybe we just went a step further a lot sooner than we should have. Maybe we should have given ourselves more time to sort everything out."

Glancing down at her beer, she shook her head. "I don't know, Garth." She raised her head. "How would we have ended differently?"

We'd come to the moment of truth, and I felt we had to face it. "I don't know that we would have ended differently. Sometimes two people, and maybe that includes us, can only go so far together, and then that's it. Partly it has to do with where each is in his life, but mostly it has to do with each other."

"Are you saying we aren't meant for each other?"

"I'm saying that perhaps we're meant to be friends. Nothing more. Nothing less. And that whatever we felt for each other beyond that was in some ways a lie. That's why it couldn't hold up over time, or even beyond a few months."

Tears came into her eyes. "But I've never loved you more than I do right now."

"But do you want to spend the rest of your life with me?"

"No. Not at this point."

"And do you want me to hold you for whatever time we have left in today?"

She glanced around at all she had left to do. "Maybe later."

Another silence followed, that one deeper than the first. Glancing around her kitchen, from the antique plates rimming it to the blue-and-white wallpaper to the wine rack to the brick wall of the fireplace, I realized

**225**

how much I'd come to miss it, how much more I'd miss it in the years to come.

"Garth, what's going to happen to Devin?" she asked.

I thought of Devin and Jenny. After short stays in the hospital—Devin for a concussion, cracked ribs, and a dislocated shoulder, and Jenny for exposure—Devin LeMay and Jenny Carter were then taken to jail by the Madison police. Accompanied by Rupert and me, Diana had filed charges earlier that day against both of them for kidnapping and confinement. On my own best advice I didn't report the murders of John Knight and Helen Carter LeMay. I hated Devin LeMay. Had I been able, I would have seen him tried for murder and executed. But only one person could hang him, and that was Jenny Carter. I thought I knew her well enough to know that she would lie through her teeth, perhaps even go to prison if necessary, to do just the opposite. It wouldn't help my cause any to have him tried for murder and acquitted. Because of the law regarding double jeopardy, that would only free him from the possibility of ever being charged with those murders in the future. I wanted something to hang over Devin LeMay's head. So John Knight and Helen Carter LeMay were buried side by side in McCorkle Cemetery, where I hoped they'd find more peace than they had in life.

"I don't know what'll happen to Devin," I said in answer to her question. "But you'll have to testify against him. And that won't be easy."

"Easier than you think," she said with resolve. "He not only betrayed my feelings for him; he also made a fool out of me."

"You feared him, didn't you?" I asked. "That's why you dreaded to go up north with him."

"I didn't exactly fear him," she answered. "But

sometimes, not often, but sometimes, I saw something in his eyes that disturbed me." She gathered her feet up under her. "It was as if they belonged to somebody else, and he had no control over them."

"Then why did you go ahead and go? Did you fear what he might do to you if you didn't?"

Leaning back in her chair, she said, "Yes. Not that I really thought he would do anything to me. But something inside me said he might." She seemed to have a hard time accepting the fact that she'd made a mistake about Devin. "You know I'm usually a pretty good judge of character."

"I know. So am I. But Devin is a damn good actor."

"A damn good something," she said angrily. She rose to get us another beer. On her return she said, "You could answer one last question for me. If not Devin, who made those obscene phone calls to me?"

"My guess is Jenny Carter. She loved Devin and hated you. So she found a way to let you know how she felt."

She sighed as she wrapped her arms around me and held on tight. "I had such a good life up until then. I really did. How did I ever get in that mess in the first place?"

"Do you really want an answer?"

"No," she admitted. "I don't."

"I didn't think so."

She straightened, resting her hands lightly on my shoulders. "You know, I could really use some help around here tonight. Why don't I put on a pot of coffee, and you can build a fire, even though we don't need one, and when we get done, I'll give you the best back rub of your life there in front of the fire."

"It's a deal," I said.

227

She smiled. "We weren't all that bad for each other, were we? Didn't we have some good times?"

I smiled back at her. If we lived to be a hundred, that smile of hers would still turn me inside out. "We did at that," I agreed.

# 19

*I* left at twilight, nearer dark than dawn, though the rose promise of dawn glowed in the east. Oakalla was still tucked in for the night, its streets and sidewalks empty, its stores and houses dark, its people too much at home to hurry to get somewhere else. Just a sleepy one-horse town in south-central Wisconsin with no real claim to fame. My town just the same.

I met Rupert driving up the street as I was walking down it. He stopped his patrol car and rolled down the window.

"Nice morning for a walk," he said, knowing where I'd been.

"It's a nice morning for anything," I agreed.

He waved me to one side, then spat into the street. "You know one thing's been bothering me for a while," he said. "Whatever happened to John Knight and Devin

229

LeMay's wife, Helen? You haven't said a word on the subject since you've been back."

"One of life's unsolved mysteries," I answered with a straight face.

"I'll bet," he said. Then his eyes skewered me. "How bad was it?"

"Bad enough that Doc Airhart had never seen anything like it."

He spat again. "I figured it was something like that. But don't you think their families have a right to know?"

"I'm working on that," I said. "As soon as I can figure out a way, I'll tell them."

"While you're at it, tell them who did it."

"I'd like to," I said.

Taking out his chew, he tossed it into the gutter alongside a beer tab and a cigarette butt. "He'll never serve that first day in prison. You know that, don't you, Garth? He'll either lie or charm his way out of it. Or plead insanity and have himself committed."

"I know that, Rupert."

"So why didn't you throw him off that roof while you had the chance?"

"I won't say I didn't consider it."

He put his patrol car in gear. "Well, I hope we both don't live to regret it."

I nodded, as the patrol car started to roll. "Give my regards to Elvira," I said.

"When I get home."

Ruth sat at the kitchen table in her slippers and robe with bags under her eyes and a cold cup of coffee in front of her. From all appearances she'd been up longer than I had.

"I suppose there's no use asking where you've been," she said.

"At Diana's."

Her brows rose slightly. "I see."

"To say good-bye," I added.

"Short-term or long-term?" she asked skeptically.

"Long-term."

Relief spread over her like the glow of hot rum. "It's about time."

"I wish I felt the same."

"You will," she said, rising to pour us each a cup of coffee. "In time."

While she puttered about the kitchen in preparation for breakfast, I retrieved the photograph I'd taken from Devin LeMay's house right before the police arrived. Laying it on the table in front of me, I sat studying it until I attracted Ruth's attention.

"What are you doing?" she asked.

"Trying to solve a puzzle."

She leaned over my shoulder to look at the photograph. "What kind of a puzzle?"

"The what's-wrong-with-this-picture? kind of puzzle. For the life of me I can't figure it out."

Breakfast was momentarily forgotten as Ruth sat down in her chair and took the photograph from me. Seconds later her face registered recognition, then disbelief. She was at a loss for words—a first, or at the least, a second for her. "Do you know who this is?" she asked, still staring at the photograph in disbelief.

"Devin LeMay and his mother. Why?"

"Oh my God," she said, closing her eyes and hanging her head. "Would I have known."

"What's wrong, Ruth?"

She opened her eyes to look at me. I couldn't tell if her tears were of joy or of sorrow, or of something in between. "Where and when was this photograph taken?" she asked.

"The where I don't know. My guess is Devin

231

LeMay's house, which actually belonged to Esther Mc-
Corkle. It's the when that's been bothering me. That
looks like a forties photograph, with Devin saluting in
his sailor suit and all. But it can't be, not if he's
thirty-four, like Jenny Carter said."

"It is the forties, Garth," she said. "I'd bet my life
on it."

"How do you know?"

"Because that girl in the picture, whether she's
Devin LeMay's mother or not, is Hattie McCorkle."

I took the photograph from her, though she wasn't
sure she wanted to give it up. "You couldn't be mistaken?"

"No, Garth," she said with certainty. "I'm not
mistaken. I know that face almost as well as I know my
own. I should. I've seen it enough over the past fifty
years."

"Then Devin LeMay isn't thirty-four," I said.

"More like forty-five."

"I shouldn't be so surprised. Henry McCorkle himself said that the McCorkles didn't show their age. All
except Esther, he said, which explains why she could
pass for Hattie's mother later on." I handed the photograph back to Ruth. "Where do you suppose Hattie
went after she escaped from the church basement?" I
said.

Deep in thought, Ruth had all her feelers out. Even
her arched eyebrows looked like antennae. "I don't
know where she went," Ruth said. "But I can guess
where she ended up."

"Home?"

"That would explain why people thought they saw
her every now and again along Lost Road. Why nothing
more about her appeared in the paper."

"You looked through the back issues, too. I won-

232

dered why you were so anxious to sit with the *Oakalla Reporter* that day. But," I said, taking my first drink of coffee, "why wouldn't Esther McCorkle have said anything, particularly to you?"

"For the reason you mentioned earlier. Without suitors for Hattie, Esther wouldn't run the risk of losing that property she had her sights set on."

"And Simon McCorkle? Why was he content to keep it quiet?"

"For the same reason Hattie McCorkle killed him."

That took a moment to sink in. When it did, I didn't like the taste of it. "Do you think Simon wanted Hattie right there at home with him for as long as he needed her?"

"What do you think?" she asked.

"I think I'd rather not think too hard about it," I said. "Or who Devin LeMay's father really was."

"Maybe the huckster that Esther ran off with wasn't the real father of her child either," Ruth said. "That's why he kept on going and Esther came back."

"So then, who did kill Simon?" I asked. "Esther or Hattie?"

"I'm betting on Hattie," she said. "If Simon McCorkle did get her pregnant, she'd have good reason. Besides, the more I think about Hattie McCorkle, the more I realize just how much like her son she was. She had her share of the wolf in her, too, Garth, pretending to be totally helpless when all the time she was using it to bend people to her will." Ruth glanced down at the photograph of Hattie McCorkle and Devin LeMay. "But I would have liked to have seen the look on her face when she realized too late that instead of her son's jailer, she had become his prisoner."

"Do you think she drove him to become what he was?" I asked.

233

"I think she helped. But I also think it was in his blood from the beginning. Nobody else can drive us that far off course."

"Hattie might have killed Simon by herself. But she would have needed help hanging him on that hay hook," I said.

"And you think it was Esther who helped?"

"Who else?"

She shook her head, apparently disgusted at herself. "Even so, I had Esther pegged wrong all these years. Her only crime was being a McCorkle, and trying too hard to change everybody else's spots."

Taking the photograph from Ruth, I dropped it in the kitchen wastebasket on my way up the stairs. "See you later," I said.

"Where are you going?"

"To shave, for starters."

"It's about time," she agreed.

Minutes later, standing over a steaming bowl of water, with lather on my face and a razor in my hand, I took a good hard look at the man in the mirror across from me. Eye to eye we stared back at each other until he finally broke into a grin. He never could take himself too seriously. For that matter, neither could I.